"In *London Skin & Bones*, a corner of the past comes alive, regenerates flesh and muscle, and throws on a coat (with a freshly-rolled joint tucked in its pocket) to wander a neighborhood populated by an unlikely, diverse tribe of friends who weave in and out of stories with familiarity so warm you'll wonder if these tales came from your own memory—or your own dreams. Ian Young knows you can fall in love with a city with the same enthusiasm and eroticism you fall for a person, and deep in blue-collar London of the 1980s, with its eclectic shops and sporadic downpours, its veterans and refugees of other countries' wars, its confident sexuality rising like a collective adolescence, an easy mingling occurs. Reading these stories, you're not a stranger in a strange land. You're a traveler welcome to a cup of something warm or something strong, someone's hand tapping lightly on your shoulder with an invitation to join the next spectacular adventure right around the corner."

—Bryan Borland, author of
DIG and *Less Fortunate Pirates*

"Like Isherwood's 'I Am a Camera' *Berlin Stories*, Young's interlocking London stories of Lad Culture, told by a book-loving ex-pat photographer, are droll mugshots of boxers, shop boys, immigrant gangsters, stoned philatelists, and their older tor/mentors who survived the 1940s Blitz easier than 1980s Thatcherism. A marvelous book! Quoting Noel Coward, 'I couldn't have liked it more!'"

—Jack Fritscher, PhD, author of
Mapplethorpe and *Gay San Francisco*

"Ian Young gives us a wonderful sense of a particular time and place in 1980s London, but he does so much more than simply that. His fascinating cast of skinheads, scoundrels (charming ones at that), collectors, and eccentrics turns the cliché of the 'city as character' on its head, reminding us of a neglected truth: that a city is its people, that the flow of beautiful, flawed and fascinating people is what gives a town, and a life, its texture and vitality.

Even better, he shows us this in interwoven vignettes that are as unfailingly delightful as they are edifying."

—Peter Dubé, author of
The City's Gates and *Beginning with the Mirror*

"In 1980, Ian Young came to live in an area of north London where we so-called Londoners never thought of setting foot. We made a big mistake! Resident there was a colony of more colorful figures than could ever be imagined—refugees, skinheads and shopkeepers, decent, kindly, humorous, perhaps not always absolutely honest folk (Russell the landlord ran the Blind Guide Dogs charity racket), enduring a repressive Tory government but determined to live life to the full. Young is not the first London chronicler since Dickens to use the short-story format, but the time has come to put the earlier books up for a while and settle down with *London Skin & Bones*. All hail Ian Young, the Boz of Finsbury Park!"

—Timothy d'Arch Smith, author of
The Frankaus and *The Books of the Beast*

"Great fun getting to know the colorful inhabitants of a seedy London neighborhood where gays and gay life are, refreshingly, part of the ordinary world. The book is marvelously observed and written, and proves that when gays are seen as real people, we don't need the usual melodrama of 'being gay.'"

—Edward Field, author of
After the Fall: Poems Old and New

"Skinheads, punks, boxers, and refugees—Ian Young's 1980's Finsbury Park is ground zero for the queerest of the queer. If fiction is about character, Ian Young's stories are masterpieces, shedding light on gay life in a colorful working-class London neighborhood. Radically gay and radically political, Young is always a refreshing voice in gay letters. This is fresh fiction—unlike anything you've read. Move over Armistead Maupin's *Tales of the City*. Finsbury Park has arrived!"

—Trebor Healey, author of
A Horse Named Sorrow and *Eros & Dust*

LONDON
SKIN & BONES

ALSO BY THE AUTHOR

POETRY

White Garland: 9 Poems for Richard
Year of the Quiet Sun
Double Exposure
Some Green Moths
Invisible Words
Common-or-Garden Gods
Sex Magick
Cool Fire: 10 Poems (with Richard Phelan)
Lions in the Stream (with Richard Phelan)
Schwule Poesie (with Joachim Hohmann)
The Male Muse: A Gay Anthology (editor)
Son of the Male Muse: New Gay Poetry (editor)
Yes Is Such a Long Word: Selected Poems of Richard George-Murray (editor)
On Mallard Feet: Poems by Joseph Lipson (editor)
Curieux d'Amour by Jacques d'Adelsward Fersen (translator)

FICTION

On the Line: New Gay Fiction (editor)

NONFICTION

The Stonewall Experiment: A Gay Psychohistory
Gay Resistance: Homosexuals in the Anti-Nazi Underground
The Beginnings of Gay Liberation in Canada
Out in Paperback: A Visual History of Gay Pulps
Encounters with Authors: Scott Symons, Robin Hardy, Norman Elder
Overlooked & Underrated: Essays on Some 20th Century Writers (editor)
The AIDS Cult: Essays on the Gay Health Crisis (editor, with John Lauritsen)
The Radical Bishop & Gay Consciousness: The Passion of Mikhail Itkin (editor, with Mark A. Sullivan)

REFERENCE

The Male Homosexual in Literature: A Bibliography
The AIDS Dissidents: An Annotated Bibliography
The AIDS Dissidents: A Supplement to the Annotated Bibliography

LONDON
SKIN & BONES
The Finsbury Park Stories

IAN YOUNG

with illustrations by
William Kimber

SQUARES & REBELS
Minneapolis, MN

ACKNOWLEDGMENTS

Some of the stories in this collection were first published in the anthologies *Best Gay Stories of 2012* (Lethe Press), *Boys of the Night* (StarBooks), *A Casualty of War* (Arcadia Press), *The Mammoth Book of Gay Short Stories* (Robinson Publishing and Carroll & Graf), *Serendipity: The Gay Times Book of New Stories* (Gay Men's Press), *Speak My Language & Other Stories* (Constable & Robinson), and *What Love Is* (Arcadia Press), and in the periodicals *Callisto, Chelsea Station, Jonathan,* and *Lambda Philatelic Journal.*

My thanks to the editors of these publications, to William Kimber for providing the illustrations, to Jerry Rosco and Wulf for their editorial assistance, and to the late Richard George-Murray, who provided the title for "Take These Pearls."

DISCLAIMER

This is a work of fiction. Names, characters, businesses, places, events, and incidents are either the products of the author's imagination or used in a fictitious manner.

COPYRIGHT

London Skin & Bones: The Finsbury Park Stories.
Copyright © 2017 by Ian Young.

Illustrations by William Kimber.

Cover Design: Mona Z. Kraculdy
Cover Photograph ("Andy behind the boxing club"): Ian Young

All rights reserved. No part of this book can be reproduced in any form by any means without written permission. Please address inquiries to the publisher:

Squares & Rebels
PO Box 3941
Minneapolis, MN 55403-0941
USA
E-mail: squaresandrebels@gmail.com
Online: squaresandrebels.com

Printed in the United States of America.
ISBN: 978-1-941960-07-3
Library of Congress Control Number: 2017938008

A Squares & Rebels First Edition.

for Wulf

* * * * *

"Why, Sir, you find no man, at all intellectual, who is willing to leave London. No, Sir, when a man is tired of London, he is tired of life, for there is in London all that life can afford."

—Dr. Samuel Johnson, 1777

"I do not at all like that city. All sorts of men crowd together there from every country under the heavens. Each race brings its own vices and its own customs ... No one lives in it without falling into some sort of crime. Every quarter of it abounds in great obscenities ... You will meet with more braggarts there than in all France; the number of parasites is infinite ... jesters, smooth-skinned lads, Moors, flatterers, pretty boys, effeminates, pederasts, singing and dancing girls, quacks, belly-dancers, sorceresses, extortioners, night-wanderers, magicians, mimes, beggars, buffoons: all this tribe fill all the houses. Therefore, if you do not want to dwell with evil-doers, do not live in London."

—Richard of Devizes, *c.* 1185

"Yesterday, in Babylon,
Tomorrow we be in Zion!
But what of today, my friend?
O my brother, what of today?"
—Reggae song, *c.* 1980

STORIES

Just Another Night in Finsbury Park ... 1

The Tall Boys Club ... 10

Flags of the Vlasov Army ... 20

A Boy's Book of Wonders ... 30

Soakers & Scavengers ... 37

The Buggery Club ... 45

The Man Who Shot Peabody Dredd ... 55

Take These Pearls ... 63

Mrs. Singh's Tandoori Popcorn ... 74

The Boy in the Blue Boxing Gloves ... 86

In My Dreams I Can Drive ... 94

Sexual Alternatives for Men ... 111

One for the Old Sarge ... 121

JUST ANOTHER NIGHT IN FINSBURY PARK

Darkness comes on quickly in the autumn evenings, and Finsbury Park—even in daytime the grayest of London districts—succumbs passively to a chilly gloom. Deserted streets become more depressing under the hard magnesium glare of silver lamps jutting from concrete pillars, too high for vandals to bother with.

London is a conglomeration of villages that have been absorbed over the centuries by the spreading city. Each has its own High Street and its own small park. Some of these districts are green and picturesque, but Finsbury Park is not one of them. Tucked into a neglected pocket of North-East London, it was a dusty, ugly district of looming Victorian and Edwardian row houses made over into flats, of oil shops and repair garages struggling to survive, of boarded-up factories and crumbling brickworks, and a few scraggly paradise bushes poking out of the dirt of neglected gardens.

At its center, gathering rubbish and wind-blown newspapers, a grimy brick and stone tube station of indeterminate age squats under a jumble of rusting bridges, like some enormous collapsed machine. Twice a day it stirs itself to life, wheezing and clanging in the crush of shuffling rush-hour crowds, and then emptying, leaving its musty passageways and dreary tunnels as desolate and lifeless as before.

On the streets off the Holloway Road, at random intervals among the tall stone houses, identical rectangular patches of grass appear, provided by the local council with one bench and one—only one—bush apiece. At the edges of these utilitarian parkettes, the walls of the remaining buildings show the paint and plaster outlines of what once were houses: for the little parks are the last of the wartime bomb sites, playgrounds now for quiet Indian children watched over by their sari-clad grandmothers.

This is the London that Thatcherism passed by—and left even more broken and depressed. It was not the worst London had to offer by any means: it hadn't sunk to the despair that wafted like a bad smell through the crime-infested filth of Brixton. It was just a gray area, a pocket for dreary weather, with an odd, unsettling quietness about it. Some of the abandoned buildings had been taken over by squatters—young, homeless, unemployed. A few storefront groceries run by Rastamen kept erratic hours selling take-out patties and bags of flour. Sikhs and Chinese stayed open a little later than anyone else. By nine o'clock, no one was on the streets, and most of the house-lights were out. Only the sweeping headlights and the swish of cars on their way to other places kept the district from appearing completely deserted.

The boarding house I lived in was the last of a line of crumbling, wedding-cake gothic piles on Turle Road. Before the bombing it had been in the middle of a row called Finsbury Mansions, but a couple of direct hits had demolished the end of the street. Part of the empty space was now a hideous secondary school, sardonically named after George Orwell. The rest served as the local cricket pitch. Some evenings indistinct figures would linger there for a while after dark, running through the thick shadows (there were no lights) and sometimes calling to one another, determined to finish their game before rain or total darkness sent them home.

That fall the evenings were especially cold and damp, and I would bundle up in my old tweed overcoat and brown wool scarf for my nine o'clock walk down High Street and through the twisting back roads, with a packet of shrimp chips in my pocket and—if it was a Friday night—(what luxury!) a precious, thinly rolled joint.

It wasn't raining when I set out, but a cool wind was springing up, blowing papers and discarded wrappers through the weeds in the boarding house garden. Fugitive newspaper pages clung to the rosebushes by the wall like crude veils. In the autumn cold I hunched against the damp English wind that gives half the population chest complaints by middle age. My friend the black and white cat wasn't at his usual windowsill perch tonight: probably inside, sensible and warm.

LONDON SKIN & BONES

I headed for a little row of shops on one of the winding back streets. The street lamps there were older, and more friendly than the penitentiary-style lighting above the main road. The shops were shut of course, most of their windows dusty and unrevealing, or lit by a single bare low-watt bulb. Heath's Tools had a front window full of secondhand engines, belt drives, and odd-looking gears. A faded cardboard sign, left over from the Sixties by the look of it, incongruously promised "Fun in the Sun" on Majorca. I cupped my hand, pressed my nose against the glass, and peered inside. Metal desks and wooden swivel chairs were piled on one another, and off to one side, a battered-looking garden gnome presided, arms akimbo. At the back a table was piled high with papers and tins. It began to spit rain.

The chemist's shop was the only one of the row, on either side of the street, with a properly illuminated window. Fluorescent lights threw a flickering glow onto tubes of toothpaste and stacked boxes of paper towels. A poster showed a well-groomed young couple, each smiling into the other's face while running along a beach, bizarrely dressed in a selection of trusses, supports, and elastic knee bandages. I thought of collaging it with "Fun in the Sun," perhaps adding a tank or two, and some picturesque beggars.

The raindrops began to get bigger and I smelled the distinctive, musty odor of rain on dusty cement. I ducked into the doorway of an Indian grocery; its windows were piled high with sacks of rice, dented tins of curried okra, and faded sample packets of custard powder and Ovaltine. From a window above the shop across the road, a light revealed a room with beige walls and a painting of a country cottage of the sort used for the tops of biscuit tins. No one seemed to be in the room. I leaned back against the doorjamb of the grocery and took the slightly bent joint out of my pocket. I was about to light it when I heard someone whistling.

The tune was familiar, a haunting, slightly melancholy dance that scurvy, syphilitic old Henry VIII had expropriated along with the monasteries, and passed off as his own. "Greensleeves"—and the metal-cleated footsteps that came with it—told me who it was even before I spotted him from my shadowy doorway.

"Andy!"

"Fuck, why'ncha frighten the life out o' me like creeping Jesus!"

"Sorry. Here, come in out of the rain and smoke a joint with me."

"Yeah, right on man. What a pissy night, i'n it."

Andy was a fellow boarder at the lodging house we called "the mansion." He was an intriguing fellow, a bit secretive, usually friendly, but a bit moody

3

and unpredictable. He was a skinhead, and I had never seen him go out in anything but regulation skinhead garb: jeans held up by black braces, work-shirt or T-shirt, work socks, and one of half-dozen pairs of Doc Martens, to which he added a trademark touch of his own, metal cleats—"the better to kick your fuckin' head in wiv." In fact, Andy was remarkably gentle by nature until the rare occasions when some real or imagined indignity to himself or another triggered his violent temper and he erupted in a reckless storm of fists, boots and fury. He worked at odd jobs, mostly on building sites and installing industrial carpeting. Like most skinheads, he took pride in being scrupulously clean.

Andy was tall like me. His lean body and strong hands constrasted with luminous, long-lashed green eyes, full lips, and prominent cheekbones. He had a sneering smile that seemed cheeky, mischievous, and appealing. With those he liked (the rest he preferred to ignore), he adopted a quiet, conspiratorial manner that assumed an immediate intimacy. He was tremendously sexy.

He joined me in the shop doorway and turned down the collar of his leather jacket.

"Sid came round today," he said, dragging on the joint. "We went for a ride in his car, out to his place. Ever been out there?"

"I have indeed," I said as he blew the smoke into the street. "Nice house he has. Epping, isn't it?"

"Yeah. Epping, near the forest."

"I don't know why he keeps it so gloomy though. The dining room and the front room look as though he never goes into them. I don't think he ever opens the curtains either. Bit creepy. He's a funny bloke."

Sid Brown was a fiftyish Jewish stockbroker who'd gone into early retirement so he could write and live an openly gay life. Somehow he hadn't gotten around to doing much of either and instead had become something of a recluse, puttering about his semi-detached in a housing estate at the edge of the Forest and occasionally venturing into central London with enough money to pick up a rent-boy, which is how he'd met Andy, who was sometimes willing to supplement his wages with the right customer.

Sid had become an occasional welcome visitor to the mansion—nervous, funny, a little seedy, and alternately miserly or generous, as the mood struck him. He always wore a Gay Is Good badge pinned to his suit-jacket, and smoked constantly, usually letting the ash tumble off his lapels into his wool cardigan.

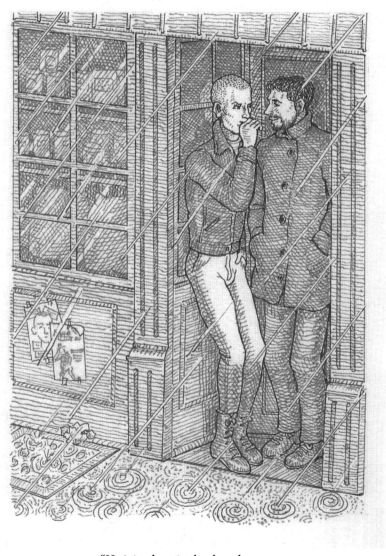

"He joined me in the shop doorway and turned down the collar of his leather jacket."

"He's got some great old boxes in that place," Andy said. Antique boxes were one of his odd interests. "You know what he said to me?" he asked, unscrewing a roach-clip that looked like a bullet. "I think he's a bit lonely out there all on his own. He asked me if I wanted to move in with him—you know, into the house in Epping like. Asked me a couple of weeks ago."

Andy looked straight into my eyes, nodding slightly, nodding, nodding, as he did whenever he wanted to be sure you were paying attention.

"Permanently?" I said, stupidly, raising my voice a bit.

"Yeah, of course!" He sounded a bit indignant. "He says I could do a bit of gardening for him and help out around the house like. Says I can type up his manuscripts for him and ... we might go into business together."

"What sort of business?" I asked as a picture of Andy with a tea towel in his hand flitted through my mind. It would certainly be a change! We were huddling together against the shop door now, Andy in his jeans and black leather jacket and me in my overcoat, sharing the last of the joint. It was strong grass and we were both getting a nice buzz.

"This is good grass, man. From the Rastas?"

I nodded.

"Financial advice," he replied to my question, with a leer that turned into a grin. I'd forgotten his chipped front tooth. "Or maybe he just wants to pimp me to wealthy gents. Anyway, it'll get me out of the mansion, won't it. Your room is all right but mine's fucking cold. And too bloody noisy by the toilet." He turned suddenly toward me and ran his fingers up my lapels, looking me straight in the face. "Here, d'you think I'm too old to do it for money?" I could see his breath and feel it, warm against my mouth.

"You're in your prime, my darling!"

"Fuck off!"

"No, seriously. If you want to do it, you can. You're good-looking, you can get all the tricks you want. Just remember though, kiddo, unless you're planning to do yourself in soon, there *is* a future to be thought of."

"Yeah, well. That's what I mean." He took a sudden look around the street as if he'd heard someone coming. "I'm sick of round here. There's nuffing for me, nuffing at all. I like old Sid. It'll be all right, moving in with him. I mean, I didn't say I would. Said I'd think about it. He was a bit pissed off, I think."

"Well, you don't want to look too eager, do you?"

"Well, no."

"Did he go down on one knee when he proposed to you?"

"Fuck off or you'll get my knee in your balls. Epping's a bit boring but I expect I'll get used to it. Not that this place is so fuckin' exciting."

"Oh, I don't know," I said. "Look, the rain's eased up. We can walk down to the laundrette and see if Mrs. Singh's cleaning the machines. She might favor us with a song or some popcorn. See, always something to do."

"Ha. Ha."

We were both buzzed by this point. I noticed Andy was wearing his tight jeans, ripped in one knee and nicely outlining his crotch. He was leaning against the shop window with his head back and his eyes closed, hands in his jacket pockets, one boot-heel hooked on the window ledge. He looked great. I leaned against him with my things around his and clasped my hands around the back of his neck; short, sharp hairs pricked my palms.

"Kiss me you fool," he ordered, his eyes shut.

His mouth felt warm and his tongue scraped against my teeth. He kept his tongue in my mouth for a long time before he broke away.

"Shit," he said, looking around. "I'm getting cold."

"Let's go home then."

"We'll go home and fuck."

Well, I thought, lucky me.

The mansion always looked odd standing at the end of the street where the row came to a sudden stop, a ragged wall showing the traces of what had once been stairways in an adjoining house. As we came near, Andy broke away and ran ahead of me onto the uncut grass, jumping high in the air and swinging his latchkey on a string over his head, not making a sound. On the back of his leather jacket he's painted a white A in a circle and SKINS RULE underneath. His small bottom look good in his tight-fitting jeans. Sid wasn't the only one who wanted to get into that ass. Andy would never let him—or anyone else.

The house looked dark from the outside but the kitchen light was on in the back, as always.

"Cup of tea, Andy?"

"Yeah, get warmed up. Be down in a minute."

It was bright in the kitchen. Electric wires and disconnected pipes hung from the ceiling and a row of new linoleum stood in one corner, ready to replace the cracked Victorian floor tiles that had worn thin, exposing the blackened wood beneath. The window over the table looked out onto a ramshackle porch that had been a greenhouse. Now it was full of old furniture, rolled-up carpets, broken bicycles and gritty flowerpots.

I put the kettle on and looked at the clock. Too late for the news. Then I saw the note pinned to the television. It was from Russell, our landlord.

Lads—gone over to gay painting show at Pink Triangle. Yes I've come over all artists all of a sudden! Frozen meat pies in the fridge, help yourselves.

Did you hear, Sid's decided to go to Australia—Sydney. Sidney in Sydney. To live with his sister, his Mum's very ill. Says he's sick of living on his own. He's put the house up for sale and all his furniture, silly bugger so I don't suppose he'll be coming back. I'm going to buy that hall-stand. Says he's got to go next week. Shall we give him a party?

The back toilet is plugged up again.

Be good I know you will!

The kettle shrieked as I took the cups off the hooks. Andy came downstairs, without his coat and shirt now, just in his jeans, braces and boots, but with his glasses on. The round, old-fashioned National Health specs gave him a strangely scholarly look. His bare chest was smooth and white, at odds somehow with his brown neck and big hands. One shoulder had a tattoo I liked, a Robertson's Marmalade golliwog waving.

"You'll come and see us—out in Epping—won't you? We'll all have tea in the drawing room. Lah di dah!"

"Of course," I said. "If it all works out." I folded Russell's note and stuck it under the radio, trying not to think too hard.

Would it have been possible? I imagined solitary, neurotic, fiftyish Sid, dithering about in a cloud of cigarette ash and suspicion, and horny, twenty-year old Andy, with his ornamental boxes and violent fits, the two of them settling into domestic bliss together among the suburban families. Pretty bloody unlikely. On the other hand, you never know. I looked out the window. The back garden beyond the greenhouse was nothing but blackness. The last cricket players had gone home; the rest of the boarders were asleep, or nowhere in sight. Only the two of us up and about now, just me and Andy, under the kitchen light. Outside the wind was springing up again, and the greenhouse windows were rattling.

"Yeah. If it works out," Andy answered. "I really like the forest, all the green trees. I like that funny wet smell the earth gets." He carried the tea mugs over to the arborite table. "Yeah, I'm getting too old for it, man. Gotta settle down. Gotta get fuckin' organized." Then without a pause: "You think old Sid would rent you a room?" And suddenly he was looking right at me again with those clear green eyes.

He was quiet for a moment. He swallowed a mouthful of tea and leaned back to tip the chair on its back legs, hooked his thumbs in his braces, and flashed his grin at me.

"Let's go to your room," he said. "It's nicer than mine." He took his glasses off and laid them gently on the table. "Is this the new tea?"

"Yes. From Russell's Mum," I reminded him. "Expensive!"

"The best, eh!" he laughed, and I laughed too. "Right on! Only the fuckin' best!"

And we headed upstairs with our half drunk tea as the damp English wind rattled the loose panes in the greenhouse door.

THE TALL BOYS CLUB

Almost as soon as I moved into Russell Hicks's rooming house in the London district they called The Park, I began to hear about the character they called—some jocularly, others rather dismissively—"the poet of the laundrettes." Though it was true that Seamus Moore was a poet, his verses —usually long and rhyming, often sarcastic and sometimes venomous— were not printed in any books or magazines that I had seen but declaimed from shop doorways and at political rallies. (These were the early days of Mrs. Thatcher's regime and in The Park she was heartily disliked and much demonstrated against.)

A week after I moved in, I hauled a duffle bag full of dirty clothes to the local laundrette and, while waiting for the rinse cycle, cast my eyes over the various notes, ads, business cards, and Lost Cat notices pinned to the crowded bulletin board. Among them was a neatly typed letter from Seamus Moore. The laundrette, dowdy, clean, and open six days a week (closed Mondays), was presided over by the plump, amiable wife of the local veterinarian, and as well as providing a necessary service to those lacking their own laundry facilities, doubled as something of a local meeting place. It was warm, there were plastic chairs to sit on, and in front of the shop, chained to an iron pipe, was a wooden bench that provided a good view of the unredeemed bomb site across the narrow street. Mrs. Singh seldom minded extra company. *And* her tandoori popcorn was a favorite local treat. (Recipe: "You just shake the fresh powder in while it pops!")

Seamus Moore, I was soon to find out, was in the habit of writing Letters to the Editor, addressed to a variety of newspapers and periodicals from the *Times* of London to *Gay News*. The letters were almost always abusive, usually beginning with some variant of "What an unpleasant, small-minded little man (or old woman) your so-called theatre reviewer (or film reviewer or editorial writer) must be." These missives would invariably characterize women, regardless of age or physical stature, as "old" and "fat"; men as "dirty" and "little." Generic abuse would then give way to more detailed complaints, often of major length. These communications were seldom accepted for publication, though the *Hampstead and Highgate Shoppers News* occasionally printed brief excerpts, invariably provoking a small flurry of communications the following fortnight as all over North East London indignant middle-aged women in cardigans took up their pens to upbraid Mr. Moore for his unacceptable, irresponsible, and indeed shameful opinions. Seamus's letters, together with any subsequent correspondence, were made available for public viewing on the laundrette notice board until officially replaced by fresh grievances. The letter that morning, intended for a Welsh poetry magazine, was typically unprintable.

I had yet to connect the author of the sarcastic notice-board letter to the man I had avoided on High Street a day or two before. I had been emerging from Featherstone's Groceteria with a heavy bag of potatoes and onions when I heard a commotion half a block away. A big, tall, raw-boned man in his fifties, with a grizzly, close-cropped, salt-and-pepper beard, and a loud voice, was shouting abuse at a rotund, middle-aged woman in a brightly colored woolen hat.

"I'd rather exchange bleatings and fartings with an intoxicated sheep than stand all morning in the public thoroughfare trading insults with some spittle-flecked old harridan." The woman, whose face I couldn't see, turned on her heel and stomped off, making a few remarks of her own, perhaps something in the order of "Who're *you* callin' an 'arridan?'"

When I got home with my groceries I mentioned the incident to Russell, my landlord, who was lying on the kitchen floor. "Oh, that'll be Seamus Moore," he said, looking up from painting a strip of wainscotting. "He's well known in these parts. His bark is worse than his bite."

"I'm glad to hear that," I said.

"He's got a bit of a temper and a lot of people give him a wide berth."

"He seemed quite abusive, I'm surprised someone doesn't take a poke at him. Or does he only pick fights with old ladies?"

"Oh, no," Russell assured me. "He'll take on anyone. He usually has a good reason but he does tend to overreact a bit." We both laughed. "The locals indulge him though 'cause he's something of local hero." And Russell proceeded to tell me *his* version of how Seamus Moore had foiled an attempted armed robbery at Mrs. Singh's laundrette.

Over the week or so that followed, I was told two or three different versions of this local legend and soon forgot whose story was whose. But the basis of what happened was the same in all versions. Apparently Seamus Moore arrived at Mrs. Singh's a minute or two after opening time one foggy morning, ready to pin one of his pronouncements to the bulletin board. To his surprise, another man was there before him, a thin, scruffy looking character in a windbreaker and Plimsolls, with a kitchen knife in his hand.

Mrs. Singh was understandably quite frightened and was telling the man there was no money in the shop that early in the day. (There was money in the cash tin on a hidden shelf behind the back counter but Mrs. Singh felt no obligation to mention it.) As the door opened, ringing its little bell, the man waved his weapon in Seamus's direction.

Seamus, as it happened, was carrying his stick that day—a handsome shillelagh (he called it a "knobkerry") of polished diamond willow with a rubber tip and a weighted head. He didn't need the stick for walking but often carried it anyway, using it to poke at things and smash the headlamps of cars whose speed or trajectory he deemed reckless.

Apparently Seamus spoke a few words to the man, standing aside and suggesting (in a tone either soothing or menacing, depending on whose version you were listening to) that it might be better if the intruder just left and then everyone could forget all about so silly an incident. The man seemed at first to concur and prepare to leave but, as he approached the door, he lunged at Seamus with the knife. Seamus, who'd been an amateur boxer in more youthful days and fortunately still had his reflexes, pulled back and suddenly alarmed Mrs. Singh by dropping to his knees on the freshly-washed linoleum. This took the intruder by surprise and as he hesitated, Seamus swung his stick into action in a wide arc, catching the man across both shins with a smart crack. The miscreant was then disarmed and thrown into the street, the door locked, and Mrs. Singh hustled out the back way to the nearby boxing club where she was made a cup of tea with a little whisky in it. From that day on, Seamus's notices were always given pride of place on the laundrette bulletin board and only permitted to be removed by Seamus himself. The intruder was never seen again.

So by the time I spotted Seamus Moore sitting on a park bench, I knew (secondhand) something of his mettle as well as having sampled (firsthand) a little of his vituperative style of public communication. I was heading home for an early dinner when I spied him. Avoiding him would have been awkward. I prepared to walk past him, assuming he had no reason to rescue, injure or shout at me. But as I drew near, he looked up from the book in his lap, flashed a broad smile, and waved me over.

"Do you have a light by any chance this fine evening?" The accent was London but the intonation suggested Ireland or Liverpool. I pulled a book of matches from my coat.

"Ah, you're a fine lad!" He dug into an inside pocket and withdrew an old-fashioned silver cigarette case. As he opened it, I saw it contained no cigarettes but rather several very large joints. "I'm sorry if you like tobacco, a filthy habit. But will you join me in a few puffs of this my own personal mix?"

"I would indeed," I said as I joined him on the bench and lit a reefer for him. He inhaled deeply and passed it to me. "This is fine Jamaican from Kenny de Jong with a bit of damiana added to smooth it out and cool it down and how's y'r father. Well, they *say* damiana's an aphrodisiac but it's never made me any more randy than I already am. I think you have to drink it as a tea for that, you might keep it in mind."

"Very nice," I said, savoring the first hit I'd had for weeks. Seamus Moore and I introduced ourselves and he asked whether I knew the aforesaid Kenny de Jong. I told him no, I'd only just moved to the neighborhood.

"Kenny works at the Lion Garage with the other Rastas, lovely fine fellas, young Kenny especially, you want to get to know them." As we sat and smoked, I got a good look at Seamus Moore for the first time. He was a big man, about 6'3", bare-headed and long-haired, broad-shouldered and imposing in what I learned was his usual garb of gray greatcoat, flannels, work socks, and black plastic sandals. As he handed me the joint I noticed he had extraordinarily large hands, heavily veined, with long, spatulate fingers and large, discolored, deeply grooved nails that splayed out, obscuring his fingertips. He had a full head of salt-and-pepper hair and hairy ears. His rather Roman nose had a pronounced dent in the middle of it.

As we sat, he pulled a paper bag from his pocket and extracted a few mixed nuts in their shells, throwing them onto the pavement. The strong, sweet grass made me feel mellow and I was soon answering my companion's questions. I told him about my long stay in Canada with my parents and how I had always returned for holidays, staying with my aunt and uncle in Barkingside. And how my last trip back had somehow extended itself so that I was now ensconced in Finsbury Park, in no hurry to return any time soon to the Land of Snow. He asked me why the Park and I told him it was the cheapest district in London that wasn't actually unsafe.

"It's a grimy old place with the paint peeling off but you'll settle in here all right." He grilled me as to whether I was a boxer (I wasn't) or a stamp collector (I was), suggesting various local drop-ins. Suddenly he lowered his voice and turned conspiratorial. "Of course, there's a filthy crowd around here too, well, not so much around here but in the *vicinity* I would say. They're not a nice crowd, not a nice crowd at all. I won't spell it out for you in all its sordid details on such a nice evening. But another time perhaps. What are you reading?"

He had noticed the paperback in my coat pocket. "Adam Diment, *The Dolly Dolly Spy.*"

"Yes, yes, good adventure yarn. Very hetero, of course, so not especially to my taste but very juicy." It was then I realized that, like me, Seamus Moore was, as he himself liked to put it, "East of Eden."

A number of black and gray squirrels had now congregated, sniffing for nuts. He began quietly talking to them. "I know all the squirrels round here," he confided. "I call that one Otter," he said, pointing to one with a long thin tail that dragged behind him. Otter came and took a peanut from Seamus's hand. "Amazing little creatures they are," he smiled, flashing a pair of strikingly blue eyes and a stained set of serrated incisors. "You'd think the way they run along the branches and telephone wires they'd have good vision," he said, "but they don't. Their sight is really pretty poor and their hearing's only so-so. They do everything by smell and touch and memory. And *reflex!*" he emphasized. "Their *reflexes* are their main defence. They're so quick they really function as an extra sense." Otter took another peanut and ran away with it. "Here's One Eye," said Seamus, and a small, one-eyed black squirrel picked up a nut from the pavement and stood on her hind legs to eat it, baring two rows of tiny teats, pink against her charcoal-colored skin. "It doesn't seem to hinder her at all," he said. "They're marvellously adaptable ... See the way she turns her nut every which way before she eats it, got to get right comfy with it, you see. They never eat the skins, you notice. Always spit them out." Sure enough, tiny fragments of peanut skin lay at the creature's feet.

After filling me in on the history, breeding, and nesting habits of squirrels, Seamus asked me if I'd eaten. I told him I was on my way home to have dinner. "You know Ali's, yes?" I told him I did indeed. Ali's was the local caff, open early with every item individually priced, from an egg to a single slice of toast to a chicken curry.

"Ali's a good bloke. He's from some godforsaken part of Pakistan which I'm sure is a fine and pleasant country. Only place you can get a breakfast in *these* parts." He thought for a moment. "Are you a religious lad?" It was nice to be called a lad still as I was already into my thirties and only my elderly dentist still regularly called me "young fella." I admitted to Seamus that no, I was not what you would call religious.

He raised his voice. "Not what *I* would call religious! What *I* would call religious is some loathsome old busybody like this Mary Whitehouse creature poking her sweaty snoot into everyone's private business." Mrs. Whitehouse was the founder of the National Viewers and Listeners Association, a network of volunteer spies pledged to root out homosexuality and other immoralities from British life. "What an unappetising old sow *she* must be! Should have had her fat, rancid arse kicked years ago! *And* her dessicated sidekicks like Muggeridge fouling his knickers every time you turn around, and that great queen Cliff Richard, they ought to know better. Not that I wish them ill, we mustn't speak ill of the dead." I was about to say something that would reveal my own membership in the East of Eden club but Seamus was on a roll and I was content to savor the good grass and soak up his diatribe. Instead of the denunciations I expected though, he started to reminisce about his youth in the far-off Fifties.

"I used to go to all the queer pubs then. Course it wasn't like now, no Gay Liberation in those days, everything illegal and all. In the blackout during the war, everyone had a right old knees-up but I was too young to know anything about it, I spent *my* adolescence hiding in a Morrison shelter reading comics and my Dad's books. The Fifties were pretty dreary, everything rationed except tablets. But I'd met this young lad, Philip, you see. A fine tall boy he was then, with beautiful curly ginger hair. Ginger, that's what they used to call queers then, for ginger beer, rhymes with queer, you see. Anyway, Phil and I had great times together, we used to spend the day in Regent's Park. I was doing a bit of boxing in them days and he'd come to watch me fight." He stroked his battered nose with a huge hand like a big cat washing its face. "We'd go to Hyde Park Corner and listen to old Bonar Thompson hold forth, he was my hero then, poor old sod."

The late Bonar Thompson, Seamus told me, was the last of the old-fashioned radical orators, standing on a soapbox, deflecting hecklers and collecting coins from the meager crowd. He wore a broad-brimmed black hat stained with sweat, and when he harangued an audience his false teeth chattered and his thin hands shivered and shook. "When I knew him," said Seamus, "his great days were behind him if you can call them that. He lived with his good lady wife in a squalid little cellar smelled of cats' piss and boiled cabbage. He was a great one for helping the poor cats was Bonar. And he was a funny old bloke. He'd say: 'On the buses there are notices saying *Spitting Prohibited: Fine Twenty Shillings*. In the British Museum there are notices saying *Spitting Prohibited: Fine Ten Shillings*. What's the moral? If you *must* spit, spit in the British Museum!' Old Bonar used to say he was neither right wing nor left wing nor any part of the political chicken. 'I'm a confirmed skeptic,' he'd say. 'I have no party, no policy, no remedy, no message, and no hope!'

"Look at those little devils!" Seamus suddenly interjected. At the base of a nearby tree, two squirrels were entwining themselves around one another like a pair of speeded-up wrestlers. "They're about to mate," he informed me. "They're very sensual, you see. They explore one another all over with their bodies and their little hands, not like dogs or cats or most four-footed creatures at all, much more like people. Quicker though." He gave a laugh and took a dented silver hip flask from the lining of his coat. He took a swig and offered it to me. "It's just a little something to keep the blood circulating. Now I used to be a drinker you see and a chain-smoker too, and if the truth were known"—here he paused and looked around as though to ensure no one was listening—"if the truth were known, I was a much nicer man when I was drinking. Oh, yes, I was a right pleasant young cove in those days, not the miserable old party with a weepy eye and a leaky bum that I am today. I can still go a round or two, though!"

He told me he'd taken to drink when his boyfriend Philip left him to join a Buddhist group. "Not that I've anything against the Buddhists, poor souls," he said. "But this guru he got in with, he was a bad lot. Scottish he was, but he'd been to Tibet so he said and claimed to be the reincarnation of some high lama or other. They called him the Rimposhay. Anyway, this lot of Buddhists had this piece of forest up in Scotland where Phil was staying so up I went on the train to see him. That cost a bit, I can tell you in them days.

LONDON SKIN & BONES

"Well, they had this big stretch of woods, very nice, just a few buildings on it. The Meditation Centre they called it. Rimpy wasn't there, just Phil and a chap who chopped the wood for the fires and this old Buddhist nun who pretty much kept to herself. Soon as I got there I knew things weren't right. Phil, he took me to this cabin, you see. *He* slept in the big house. Well, we'd always kipped in together so I knew it was going to be a bit dreary. I didn't ask any questions though. I was glad to see him. He showed me about the place and I went to my little room and made a fire and started to read these mimeographed pamphlets the Rimposhay had written. Well, what a load of bollocks! All about how Buddhism was heterosexual and such nonsense. Well, *I knew* too much for that.

"Did you *know,*" he asked, "there's a sect of Buddhism they call True Word Buddhism. It's quite queer, handsome young monks and everything, founded by a chap called Kobo Daishi in King Egbert's time, which as you well remember from *1066 and All That* was around the year 800. You can visit their temples on this famous mountain in Japan. Anyway, I thought this anti-homo stuff was just adding to our problems, you know. Course, I never was one to keep my mouth shut so I up and said what I thought which is always perilous."

"Did he argue with you?" I asked.

"Well, he *didn't*. He just tried to make excuses. It was as if he couldn't see what was printed on the page in front of him. What they call a *negative hallucination*! Well, early next morning I got up with the birds. I wasn't very happy, of course. I walked out into the woods just to clear my head and in this little clearing was this old lady, the old nun. She was sitting cross-legged on the ground, meditating, I suppose, very quiet. I didn't want to intrude but I couldn't help peeping at her through the bushes. Do you know, she was sitting stock still and squirrels were crawling all over her and after a while two little sparrows even landed on her head."

Our own squirrels were scampering and sniffing round us. "Here," said Seamus. "You want to get to know this little lot. I don't suppose the birds'll land on you like the old lady but do you know how to get a squirrel to touch you?" I shook my head. "Roll up your trouser legs!"

So there I sat in my new neighborhood, high as a kite, sharing a park bench with this strange old man (he seemed old to me at the time) and my trouser legs rolled up around my knees. I thought, if anyone comes along now, they'll think I'm a right berk. But no one did.

"Take a hazelnut," said Seamus, "and hold it on your lap."

I did as he said and a few moments later, a gray squirrel approached, climbed up my leg and took the nut from my fingers with its teeth. I felt the padded soles of its tiny, narrow feet, moist and cold on my bare skin. I looked into its shiny black eyes and it ran off with the hazelnut. Seamus looked at the squirrel. "*There!* You've made a friend!"

"Well, after that, I didn't see Phil for a long time. Course it was never the same. Well, there's some friends that come and go, and others that stay til the end. Funny thing is, you never can tell which is going to be which." He folded up his brown paper bag and put it back in his pocket. "About a year later there was a wee bit of a scandal at the Meditation Centre. Seems the Rimposhay—his real name was Dennis Monkhouse so they say—had been climbing into the sack with his young disciples—the lads I mean—and never looking them in the eye, the next morning everyone pretended it never happened. And all the time preaching being queer was a terrible thing! Well, I thought that was pretty rum. Course they hushed it all up. The things people do eh?

"I was fond of Phil. I drank quite a bit for years after that. Til I got fed up with it. I wasn't *contributing* anything, you see. I was just drinking and that was it. Now I just have a nip occasionally to warm me up and I work at the boxing club helping the lads. Here, look, there's the Grey One." A big gray squirrel climbed down a tree head first and hopped over to us. Seamus threw him a walnut as an odd noise emanated from the branches of a nearby tree. "Must be a cat around," said Seamus. "They're great mimics, squirrels. They imitate that crying baby noise that cats make. As a warning, you know. And they imitate crows too, or crows imitate them, I've never been sure which. Anyway, if you sit still and quiet, squirrels will crawl all over you. Of course," he laughed, "they do occasionally piss on you. Just a bit. To them we're just big, odd-smelling blurry things that drop food. I learned that from the old lady at the Centre. *Anyone* can be a buddha—if you don't mind being pissed on."

He suddenly changed the subject. "You've never got in the ring though?"

"God, no," I said. "*Look* at me. I'm a runner, not a fighter! My Dad did a bit of amateur boxing in the R.A.F."

"Well, you're a sensible lad," said Seamus. He suddenly assumed a pantomime Irish accent, or a real Irish accent, I couldn't tell. "Oi'm pleased

to make your acqu-*ain*-tance boyo! You pop into the boxing club any *toime.*"
He reverted to his usual London voice. "If I'm not there, ask for Tommy,
he'll show you around." He pulled a small, rather elegant silver business card
holder from a back pocket. It occurred to me that this was the third silver
container he had flourished. The cigarette case had arisen from over his
heart, the flask from somewhere near his right lung, and the card case from
the region of his left kidney. I thought: this bloke is *armored*! (I was later to
realize that all these items, and several others, were monogrammed, each
with a different set of initials. He had bought them all at market stalls and
car boot sales.) Taking his card I suddenly realized the evening had gotten
cooler and I remembered I was hungry. I shook Seamus Moore's hand; my
own lean, ordinary hand seemed small and almost frail inside his giant one.
"And welcome to Finsbury Park!" he boomed.

I thanked him for the smoke and his good wishes, put the card in my
pocket and turned to go. As I stood up, he looked me up and down. "Don't
be a stranger. Us tall boys got to stick together, you know. *And you're in the
tall boys club now, me lad!*" he shouted after me. "*Right in it!*" And he laughed
out loud as though he had just heard some great joke. I walked quickly, but
at the gentle rise that rather oddly blocked a proper view of the park from
the street, I turned around to wave goodbye to my new acquaintance. Back
to feeding his squirrels, he didn't see me.

On the way home, a stiff, cold breeze sprang up. I stuffed my hands deep
into my overcoat pockets—and found at my fingertips a generously-rolled
joint. It could only have been a present from the abusive and notoriously
vituperative Seamus Moore.

FLAGS OF THE VLASOV ARMY

London in the Thatcher years of the 1980s had seen better days. And Finsbury Park, the working-class district where I lived, was especially shabby. Its grim, crumbling Victorian row houses, the eerie silence of its evening streets, gave it an atmosphere of decrepitude, neglect, and gloom. But when I look back on that early time, I remember most the people I came to know—most of them good people, all of them struggling to get by, as I was, some of them living day to day, others lost in memories, nursing dreams. When you are young, you imagine you have nothing—yet you take so much for granted. Only later in life do you realize how lucky you've been. But one thing I appreciated, even then, was the old, green-painted shop near High Street, Boris Mostoyenko's stamp shop—with its slightly faded sign that said HOME & OFFICE—STAMPS FOR COLLECTORS, and the light that shone from the back kitchen through the glass of the front door and onto the street. We were lucky to have a place where we could always be sure of a welcome on a cold evening, a warm stove to sit by, and an enamel mug of hot, sweet tea.

It was at Boris's that I first met Henk Sonderhausen, a lanky, temperamental Dutch daredevil whose pugnacity and streak of exhibitionism were always getting him into scrapes. Henk was one of the few true bisexuals I've ever known, and his rosy cheeks and mop of blond hair endeared him to teenage girls, old ladies, and boy-fanciers wherever he went.

I met Henk on the night of the big fight. Tommy Noakes, an aging local boxer who was everyone's friend, was scheduled to fight the Finnish middleweight champion at the Park Road Boxing Club. The Finn's scheduled opponent (who had knocked Tommy out a few months before) had broken his hand, and Tommy had been drafted to take his place at the last minute. It was the one big break of Tommy's less than glorious career, and all his friends from the neighborhood were eager to see him fight the Scandinavian, who was in line to try for the European championship later in the month. Tommy himself was so excited he was having trouble sleeping and his trainer was getting more worried by the day.

The bout was scheduled to start at eight in the evening, and the stamp shop usually stayed open late. So when I walked in the door at about half past six, Boris was especially glad to see me. "My prayers are answered!"

"Yes, God sent me, Boris! What can I do for you?"

"First, you sit. Get warm. Then, while you relax, I will assign duties."

Boris's shop was a hodge-podge of three or four different shops in one. Signs taped to the front window announced "BOOKS, STAMPS, STATIONERY" and "APPLIANCE REPAIR." One side of the shop was piled with broken toasters, used record players, old electric typewriters, antique radios, and parts of unidentifiable machines. The other side was fitted out with brown-painted bookshelves. Some of these held envelopes, staplers, notebooks, packets of colored writing paper, and rolls of stout brown parcel wrapping. The rest were crammed with secondhand books, mostly of pre-war vintage. On Boris's shelves I found Madison Grant's *The Passing of the Great Race*, Winwood Reade's *The Martyrdom of Man*, Elinor Glyn's *The Philosophy of Love*, and Nicholas Roerich's *Shambala*—all of them half-buried among dusty, broken sets of the works of Henry van Dyke, H. De Vere Stacpoole, Charlotte M. Yonge, Warwick Deeping, and other bestsellers of long ago, now yellowed, foxed, chipped, and forgotten.

Toward the back of the shop was the counter, and behind it, five-foot high walls of labeled wooden drawers in rows, holding stock-cards and packets of foreign stamps, as well as coins, badges, buttons, and an assortment of other bits and pieces. Beyond was the spacious kitchen with its large round table, unmatched wooden chairs and a long, overstuffed couch, all surrounded by precarious piles of encyclopedia volumes, magazines, comics, outdated roadmaps and much-thumbed copies of *Gay Times* and *The Catholic Worker*. A narrow staircase led upstairs to the living quarters, and a heavy, metal door led to a small weed-covered yard and a shed that served as a workshop. Taped to the wall above the gas stove was a yellowing sign that said, in printed red letters, "THE TEA IS FREE." Underneath, someone had written "Sandwiches 10p." Posters, advertisements, and portraits covered the walls. An ornate gold frame held a slightly damaged painting of the Infant of Prague, crowned and solemn, hand raised in benediction.

Boris was working at the counter as I closed the shop door behind me. Dressed, as usual, in gray flannels and a ratty cardigan, he was a small, wiry man of indeterminate age, balding and rather birdlike, with an erect, military bearing, and surprising strength and stamina. A sardonic smile was his usual expression. Behind him in the kitchen I could see the identical figures of Elliot and Lionel, one of them sitting at the round table sorting through piles of old envelopes, the other standing at the stove stirring furiously.

"Elliot, it won't hurt that soup *at all* if you should stir it a little more slowly. Thank you. What was I saying? Oh, yes. When I first got to this country I could not properly say the letter 'W'. I would say 'Voolvorts' instead of 'Woolworths'! So—I taught myself by repeating every day over and over 'The wormy old wolverine of Wolverhampton'—which, you see, I was living in Wolverhampton at the time."

At the stove Elliot giggled and shook his head, and Lionel sitting at the table did the same. Handsome, disheveled boys in their late teens, they were Boris's helpers and companions, uncannily identical, with thick, dark, curly hair and long eyelashes. Somehow Boris seemed to have no trouble telling them apart but no one else ever could and how he did it remained his secret. They were apparently twins but if you referred to them as that, you would be treated to a standard short lecture from one or the other of them (or both). They were *not* twins, you would be told, but triplets. There had been a third-born, so the story went, their "baby brother" Theodore, who had died at birth, and whose brief existence on the planet they refused, on principle, to overlook. Baby brother's spirit was even represented, on special occasions, by an old, handsome and much-loved teddy bear. This being the night of the big fight, Teddy was now in evidence—parked on top of the fridge, his fuzzy head sticking out of a battered green Aer Lingus flight bag with a broken zipper.

"The wormy old wolverine of Wolverhampton ..." Boris rolled his tongue around the consonants again, accompanied by more giggles from the triplets. "I repeated that linguistic mantra over and over so many times until I *became* the wormy old wolverine of Wolverhampton! And then I moved to Finsbury Park where I speak English as perfectly as she can be spoke. *Almost!* That tea is Tesco's special blend, a particularly good lot if I may say, so drink up."

I sat myself down across the table from Lionel and sipped the hot sugary tea, flavored with the peculiar metallic taste of condensed milk, and asked Boris what I could do for him. He held one finger in the air to indicate Time Out, reached into a drawer for his tobacco-rolling machine of green canvas and rusted metal, and proceeded to create a fat cigarette. As his tongue flicked along the gummed edge of the paper, he looked over his rimless glasses and winked at me. It would help immeasurably, he said, if I would watch the shop tonight and close up at the usual hour so he and the boys could get to the fight on time. I said I would.

"Lionel, when you come to a cover that's torn," Boris instructed, "put it in waste paper and keep just the stamps. The market for torn covers I have not yet discovered. So anyway, where was I?"

"You were telling us about the war," said Elliot, who was ladling out the soup.

"The *war! Pah!*" Boris raised his voice, spitting flecks of saliva into the air. "A nightmare from beginning to end, the war! Well, the whole of Europe was experimenting with government by the mentally ill! I was ..." he said, lowering his voice and turning in my direction. "I was in the Polish army. Then Stalin invaded Poland and I was in the Soviet army. And then I was captured by the Germans and put in a bloody camp. And I wanted to get out of the camp any way I could and ended up with General Vlasov. You know who was General Vlasov?"

Elliot interrupted to point to an old, framed black and white photo of a horse-faced man in rimless glasses and a military uniform. "That's him, isn't it?"

"That's him. If ever there was the right man at the wrong time, that was him!"

Apparently Boris and the other Russians could get out of the camp if they joined General Vlasov's turncoat Russian army.

"Vlasov was one of Stalin's best generals," Boris told us. "And not many of *them* survived the purges. He kept Hitler out of Moscow and then was too daring for his own good and got captured. The Germans let him head up a Russian liberation army made up of all us rag-tag and bobtail and flotsam and jetsam from the conquered territories. What Vlasov had in mind, you see, was to fight Stalin *and* Hitler—and Russia would be free again. *Again?*

What am I saying? Anyway, that was the idea and we had about one chance in a thousand of pulling it off."

Now Elliot was spooning bits of carrot out of his soup bowl into Lionel's, and they were both watching Boris.

"By that point, Hitler was getting his behind kicked good and hard, and Stalin's armies were driving the Nazis back into Czechoslovakia. And we went with them and ended up in Prague in the Spring of '45." Boris glanced at the clock. "Prague was held by the SS and the Russians were advancing fast. That's when we Vlasov men surprised everyone. In May we rose up and attacked the SS, drove them out of Hradcany Castle, ran up the Imperial Russian flags we'd made, and chased the Germans out of Prague. And that was the only day of the whole bloody war that I actually enjoyed ... Come on boys, eat up. I refuse to be late for the fight."

"Someone said you were a war hero," one of the Triplets said cheerily.

"They were most ill-informed! I was no such thing!" Boris answered. "I was a hunted man. I, Boris Mostoyenko, was chased across Europe like a rat and only escaped by the skin of my teeth. History issued one of its wicked decrees—and instead of heroes we were traitors! Churchill and Roosevelt did a deal with Stalin, you see. And Stalin insisted that all the Vlasov men be handed over to be shipped to Siberia in the boxcars they were no longer using for Auschwitz."

Of course we all wanted to know how Boris got away.

"Fortune smiled on handsome young Boris." He tipped his head back and smiled. "I had a tiny affair with a rather good-looking English officer. And the Englishman got wind of what was up and warned me. To him and to God I owe my life. But I found out later there were Vlasov men on the run all over Europe—with every soldier and policeman on the lookout. So much for our great enterprise to save Mother Russia! We ended up scurrying like rats in the ruins! *I, Boris Mostoyenko, lived in a pigpen! In a pigpen! For a week!* And your old Boris ended up in Vienna where Marcus Grumbacher was with the Allied Control Commission—and he got me out, thank God."

So that was where Boris had met the distinguished Marcus Grumbacher. I had met Marcus several times—a portly, well-dressed Liechtensteiner with silver hair, an evaluator of rare coins and (Boris had confided in me one day) the silent partner behind Boris's shop.

"What happened to General Vlasov?" I wanted to know.

Boris Mostoyenko looked right at me, paused for dramatic effect, and slowly spoke. "General Vlasov," he said, "was one of those men who gambled with history—and lost. Stalin hanged him."

The soup bowls were piled in the sink and Boris and the Triplets headed off to the Boxing Club, carrying Teddy in his flight bag. And I was left alone in the shop to look through the bookshelves and stamp packets, to stroke Tom, Boris's mouse-catching housecat, to browse through the musty old books and make cups of tea. There were few customers.

As I was standing behind the shop counter toward closing time, I came across an old leather-bound album with photos of a younger Boris in what looked like a tiny chapel, stripped to the waist, and enacting each of the stations of the cross. Then the little bell on the shop door tinkled. I looked up, and in came Henk Sonderhausen.

He was a tall, slim youth with a mop of blond hair, a wide mouth and a fair, apple-cheeked complexion. He wore a long army greatcoat that came down to the top of his Doc Martens, a slightly wilted yellow rosebud in his lapel, and a long, striped woolen scarf. When he saw me, the little frown on his face turned into a grin.

"Is Boris here?"

"No, he's gone to a boxing match. I'm sitting in for him. Can I help you?"

"I come to pay my debt," he said and took a handful of change from his pocket. "I bought one of Boris's famous Cinderella packets and didn't have quite enough. So here's the rest." He placed a pair of twenty pence pieces on the counter.

"I'll make sure Boris knows you came in, " I said, slipping the coins into an envelope. "What's your name?" I wrote it on the packet. "Those Cinderella packets are great, aren't they? What did you get?"

"Some Touva triangles and lots of South Moluccan birds and flowers—and these, I don't know what they are."

From the pocket of his greatcoat he took Boris's paper and glassine envelope with the drawing of Cinderella trying on the glass slipper, and removed three small, simply printed rectangles.

"I know what these are. Reproductions of old stamps from the Papal States."

"Are they forgeries?" he asked. He appeared to like the idea.

"Not forgeries exactly ... reprints." I told him my name and stuck out my hand, which he pumped vigorously for a few seconds.

"It's getting cold out," he said.

"How about a cup of tea? It's about time for me to close up."

He wrinkled up his pert little nose, which was slightly red. "I've got a better idea," he said. "I'll buy you a hot cider at that pub around the corner."

"Oh, you've discovered that! You're not from around here though, are you?"

"I'm from Holland," he said. He had only a trace of an accent. "But I'm living in Ilford. I work in the riding school in Wanstead."

I imagined him atop a horse, galloping across the countryside, hair and scarf blowing romantically in the wind. "A cider sounds good! Let's go."

As we walked to the pub, Henk unbuttoned his coat in spite of the chilly evening air. Beneath it, he had only a flannel shirt and a very tight pair of skimpy cotton shorts showing an ample bulge at the crotch. His thighs were milky white with little blond hairs. He grinned at me and I noticed the wide gap between his gleaming front teeth. "I like to show off!" he confided, and we both laughed. Well, I thought, he's certainly different as well as cute. And friendly!

To my surprise, the Four Kings was already packed when we arrived. Everyone seemed to be talking and laughing, and the place was full of smoke. As we pushed our way through the customers, I heard my name called loudly from one of the booths.

"*Me fellow poet!*" I looked in the direction of the booming voice and saw Seamus Moore, surrounded by the Triplets and a few other locals. "Here he is, and a friend with him as tall as hisself!" Seamus roared, though he was a head taller than both of us. He reminded us all, from time to time, that he was descended from "the famous Thomas Moore, the Irish man of letters" whom none of us had heard of. A large, raw-boned man with a beret, a gray beard and a full set of menacing yellow teeth, he was a pub regular who would only occasionally allow me to pay for my drink, and never minded that I ordered Coke.

"Boys, you missed the fight of a lifetime!" he shouted over the din. "Tommy took a terrible pounding from the Finn for the whole of three rounds but he never would go down. Then half a minute into the fourth, someone in the other corner yells out and the Finn turns and answers back. *Answers back he does!* And as he turns his head, old Tommy sees his opening and takes it by God! Tommy never could fend off the blows so well but he's

"And so we ran as fast as we could through the empty streets."

got one good punch, that fine left hook on the rare occasion he can find a chance to use it, and he used it tonight, boys! *Down* went the Finn and never got up till the count was over! Oh, it was beautiful, I never seen anythin' like it! What are you boys drinking?"

"Cider!" Henk and I said together, and joined in the general jubilation as Seamus made his way to the bar.

Henk and I wanted to talk but it was difficult to hear ourselves in the pub so after about twenty minutes we decided to make our exit. We said hello and goodbye to Boris, and to the battered Tommy, who was breathlessly asking everyone, "Did you *see* me, did you *see* me?" and stepped outside. At some pubs, the life inside overflows onto the street, but at the Four Kings, as soon as the doors shut behind you, the noise and light and warmth all suddenly ceased, and there you were again, back in the dark, damp silence.

We were just about to head out when Seamus Moore clambered through the pub door and wrapped a huge arm around my shoulders.

He leaned toward me conspiratorially, his beard tickling my neck, his breath smelling of beer and tobacco. "You know me, friend," he whispered. "We're all glad our Tommy won tonight. But *how many of them actually put money on him? Eh?*"

It hadn't occurred to me. Very few, I'd suppose. As the local boy, Tommy was the sentimental favorite, but the odds against him had been long indeed.

"*Well, I did!*" confided Seamus. He took a roll of bills out of his coat pocket. He peeled two off. "You and your tall friend have a few on me to make up for missing the fight!" After giving me a wet kiss on the ear, he turned away and aimed himself at the pub steps.

We hadn't walked more than a few blocks when Henk decided he had to take a piss. Instead of finding an obscure spot, he just stopped where he was—in front of the concrete wall of Latif's Service Station. He unbuttoned the appealing khaki shorts and leaning on the wall with one hand, took aim with the other, all the while grinning at me and talking about how to get to Ilford.

We were a few yards down the street when we heard a shout behind us. Running from the service station were its owners, the Latif brothers Winston and Mohammed. Winston, the older, larger and less unpleasant of the two, was bringing up the rear, and little Mohammed was charging ahead along the street yelling, "*You piss on my wall! You piss on my wall! I charge you to the police!*"

And so we ran as fast as we could through the empty streets, hopping over puddles and dodging around corners, past the cemetery wall and the closed stores, Henk's greatcoat flapping in the wind around his delicious naked legs, until we knew the Latif brothers would never find us. Then we collapsed on the little wooden bench outside the dusty windows of Mrs. Singh's laundrette, out of breath, laughing, and holding each other's arms.

We sat there for a while, getting our breath back, and talked for a bit about the pub and the fight, and then just sat quietly, at first gazing across the street, then looking at one another.

"You dropped something," I said, and picked up a bit of paper—the torn-off corner from an envelope—that had fallen out of Henk's pocket.

"Oh, thanks. That's off a letter from my pen pal in Czechoslovakia."

I looked at the stamp—an engraving of the same Hradcany Castle Boris had helped liberate from the Nazis years before. I was about to say something when Henk put his hand lightly over my mouth, reached inside his overcoat, and pulled out a little bottle in a brown leather cover.

"Rum!"

I took a sip and felt it warm my insides as I watched this tall, handsome boy perform a delicate pantomime. As we sat close together, Henk flung open his coat; I could see the wooden slats of the bench gently flattening his naked thighs. I brushed my fingers against the little blond hairs on his legs and wondered why he didn't have goosebumps as the night air was getting cold.

He took my hand in his big, smooth, long-fingered hand, and cupped my palm over his crotch. As he leaned back against the grimy window and took a swig of rum from the little bottle, the soft warm in my hand stiffened under my fingers, his eyes closed, and a long, satisfied sigh drifted from his pink, parted lips and floated out to dissipate in the drab darkness of the street.

We were halfway home by the time it started to rain.

A BOY'S BOOK OF WONDERS

In the early Eighties, when I told people I lived in Finsbury Park, they sometimes assumed I was sleeping rough, like Colin Wilson spending his nights in a sleeping bag on Hampstead Heath while he was writing *The Outsider.* There *was* a park in Finsbury Park but I seldom went into it; Hampstead Heath and Epping Forest were my wandering places.

In those days, the district of Finsbury Park was a scruffy, working-class part of North-East London with a high quota of squatters, Indians, Rastafarians, old age pensioners, and young single lads. I moved there because I could afford the reasonable rent Russell charged for the big, top floor room in his house, a Victorian mansion officially divided into "holiday flats" to get around the strict rent laws in case someone had to be quickly evicted. Fortunately, evictions were rare; Russell, who had made his down payment as a con man running a phony guide dog scheme in Australia, was a good judge of people, rented only to those who gave off the right vibes, and kept friction among the tenants to a minimum. He liked me, and I paid the rent on time. What I needed was a full-time job.

I had managed to land a temporary position at the London and Manchester Sanitary Packing Goods Company, located on the second floor of a crumbling turn-of-the-century office building on the dreary Holloway Road. The man I was filling in for was convalescing from some unspecified illness and would be returning in a month, or two months, or three.

In the meantime, the L&M suited me fine. My work answering letters, typing invoices, and organizing receipts filled most of the morning. After

LONDON SKIN & BONES

lunch at Ali's café, I could spend the afternoons writing articles and book reviews to supplement my meager wages, and nursing the Byzantine filing system. The office was presided over by Mr. Bayliss, a gentle, quiet man with a dyed comb-over who spent most of the day sitting in his cubicle of walnut and frosted glass, warming his crippled, carpet-slippered feet by a small electric fire. The unofficial—and indispensable—office manager was my friend Rose Madder, a tiny woman who chain-smoked, always wore slacks and never went out without a beret. Her face was wrinkled and lined like an old chestnut. Over her favorite gin and orange at The Four Kings she used to say she showed "all the wear and tear of them other three kings—smoking, drinking, and fucking!"—and she would hack out a loud, rasping laugh at her own expense.

Rose was a painter—mostly of small, vaguely creepy abstracts that didn't sell. Long ago she had changed her original, ordinary surname to Madder, as she thought having the same name as a paint color would be more memorable. It was, but it hadn't helped her sell her paintings. In the twenty years since she was hired as a clerk-typist, Rose had become indispensable to the efficient functioning of the L&M and particularly to Mr. Bayliss. And the L&M being one of those fusty, antiquated English companies that somehow mysteriously survived in spite of their avoidance of modern business practice, both Rose and Mr. Bayliss would probably be there forever. But I would not. I was keeping my eyes open for another position that wouldn't leave me exhausted by the end of the day.

"You should talk to the Old Sarge," Russell suggested one morning as we collected breakfast eggs from the henhouse in the back garden. "Armed Forces Surplus," just off the Holloway Road. "You never know. At least he'll sell you a cheap pair of pants."

The Old Sarge ran a shop with tables and racks of sold secondhand armed forces clothing, and equipment—British army issue khaki trousers, West German singlets, Yugoslav jackets, Canadian greatcoats, and an array of military shirts, boots, backpacks, rucksacks, mess tins, and bits and pieces at prices affordable to the local workers, skinheads, punks, Rastas, and other assorted denizens of Finsbury Park.

Sarge was a former British army quartermaster sergeant, a broad-shouldered cockney of about sixty with a ready laugh, a cough as bad as Rose's, and a friendly mongrel dog called Soldier. After a few months and with a recommendation from his friend Boris, I was hired to staff the shop

31

in the afternoons and early evenings; "You have all the qualifications for this job," Sarge used to say. "You're honest and you show up on time!" But for the first few months, I was on the bottom of the call list for Sarge's scavenging trips. One or two nights a week Sarge and a couple of lads would pile into Sarge's old lorry and troll around different areas of London looking for garbage to expropriate.

"Grab that chair, lads," Sarge would bark.

"What about the chest?"

"Too broken up, leave it," and we'd move on to the next pile, which might offer up books, or china, or discarded appliances, or old copies of *Country Life*.

Sarge's crew usually drew on several local worthies: the Triplets (Elliot and his identical brother Lionel); Yob and his friend Orbit, who lived in an abandoned house off the Seven Sisters Road; and a pale young hunchback with big dark eyes and a lopsided grin who called himself Piers Dragonheart, wore bright shirts and a Portuguese shepherd's capote, and, though he hung out with our gay crowd, only fancied the girls.

Riding with Sarge was a good way to make a little money, and if someone couldn't be reached or didn't show up, I sometimes filled in on the scavenging team. On my first outing, I crouched in the back of the lorry with Orbit, a muscular kid with a vague manner and a clouded eye. His wardrobe seemed to be supplied entirely by Sarge, except for a long, striped scarf, a Christmas present from Boris. Sarge liked to have him along as he was surprisingly strong and could even lift quite large pieces of furniture by himself.

My memories of scavenging outings with Sarge have blurred into one another, but I remember my first trip very clearly because I was trying to reconnect with someone I'd met a few nights earlier—a mysterious young guy called Harry Telford.

In those days I often used to go to the bars and clubs around Earl's Court, usually on Saturday nights. If I was still alone by the end of the evening, and the weather was good, I would walk up Earl's Court Road, along Holland Walk to Holland Park Avenue and through Notting Hill to the West End. From there I could make my way by bus and by foot back to Finsbury Park. I always enjoyed those long nighttime walks through the safe, familiar London streets, finally getting home to Turle Road by dawn, to sleep and laze through much of Sunday until it was time to go to dinner at my aunt and uncle's. And one summer night on Holland Walk, I met Harry.

Holland Walk is a long pedestrian pathway lined with grass and trees, hugging the side of Holland Park between Kensington and Notting Hill. It was usually pretty deserted but that night soon after I entered the walk from Kensington High Street, I noticed a young man perched on the edge of the park bench. He had a half-length tweed coat, curly brown hair, and a fresh, apple-cheeked look whose suggestion of innocence was belied by the smoke rings emanating from a rather large joint he was smoking. He grinned as I approached, and as I slowed down, he offered me a smoke. Without saying a word, we sat together under the lamps in the cool garden, I in my regulation leather jacket, he in his tweed and corduroys. My eager walk home interrupted by a silent, shared smoke with an attractive stranger, I soon lost interest in everything except the grass (which was strong but strangely mellow, as though mixed with damiana), the trees by the straight path, and the face of my new companion, who had closed his eyes and seemed to be in a headspace of his own as his fingers rested ever so lightly on my arm.

Harry Telford lived with his much older sister, he said, in Camden Town, as far away from Holland Walk as were my Finsbury Park digs. Before we parted that night (for it was very late and we were both tired), we promised to meet again. When I got back to my room, I carefully copied his phone number into my book before I crawled into bed.

For several days Harry and I played phone tag, getting no answer or busy signals or leaving messages with third parties. I was frustrated, and beginning to lose heart. And when I called—again—from Armed Forces Surplus, Sarge offered some unexpected advice.

I was helping him to sort a shipment of Air Force shirts and grumbling about not being able to get hold of my new friend. Sarge had been picking brass buttons out of a tin and sewing them onto a Canadian army greatcoat. Soldier slept in his basket beside the electric fire. Sarge suddenly turned to me and pointed a finger.

"You got to visualize harder!" He laughed quickly and coughed into his handkerchief. "I didn't say 'Get harder,' I said, 'Visualize harder'!"

"Well, " I said, "I've only met him once and ... well, he's a bit blurry."

"A blurry boy?"

"Afraid so."

"Just concentrate," said the Sarge. "Concentrate on that handsome face, kiddo. *You'll* find him!"

That night I headed out with Sarge, Soldier, and Orbit on the scavenger patrol.

We headed out around eleven o'clock and made for St. John's Wood, a posh area where my bookseller friend Tim d'Arch Smith lived and where Sarge said the pickings were often good. As it happened, we rescued a big box of auction catalogues, a pewter jug, and an old walnut table that took up most of the back of the lorry. And, toward the end of the run, we came across a paper bag with about a dozen old books in it. Most of them were mildewed or badly water-damaged but near the bottom of the bag there was one in surprisingly good condition. Oddly I had seen another copy of it before, when I was a kid. It was a big book of illustrated stories for boys published in the 1920s called *A Boy's Book of Wonders*. The cover, in red imitation leather, showed an embossed drawing of the top half of a teenage boy, gazing upward toward an improbably dramatic shooting star. The picture was beautifully executed and the boy unusually attractive with a slightly upturned nose, curly hair poking from under a tweed workman's cap, and a knitted turtleneck pullover with broad horizontal stripes. The book's raised design emphasized the knit of the pullover, inviting the reader to run his fingertips over the embossing.

We got back to Sarge's shop about one in the morning, and he was happy to give me *A Boy's Book of Wonders* instead of payment for the trivial amount of work I'd done. Orbit scuttled off to his squat with his Pound payment, and I headed home to sleep; I had work at the L&M the next day.

All the next day at work I tried to take the Old Sarge's advice to visualize Harry Telford. But whenever I tried to picture him, the oddly similar face of the boy on the book cover kept intruding until I could no longer tell them apart. *And* Harry still wasn't answering his phone.

"What's the matter, dear?" asked Rose as we finished work for the day.

"Communication problems," I said, hanging up the phone.

Rose laughed and gave her usual advice.

"Have a little drink, say a little prayer!"

I had dinner at Ali's that evening. Ali's was one of the few eating establishments in Finsbury Park—a workmen's café that did most of its trade in the early morning and in the evening after work. Ali was a beefy, bald, irrepressibly good-natured Indian. He liked me because I had heard of obscure Indian states like Faridkhot, Kishangar, and Rajpeepla, and even knew where they were. One evening I'd shown him the stamps from my collection; his eyes lit up as though I'd brought him the Crown Jewels.

None of the usual crowd was in attendance that night but Ali was in a particularly expansive mood (his sister was coming to visit from the old country, he said) and he gave me an extra tin of lemonade to take home in my pocket.

I made yet another call to Harry Telford at about nine o'clock: still no answer. I decided to walk to the Roundhouse.

North on the Archway Road, the Roundhouse had been built in the 1920s as a petrol station in the Art Deco style then the latest fashion. It never recovered from the hard times of the Depression and the War and was eventually converted into a downmarket coffee bar with peeling paint and frequently blocked drains. But as it had the virtue of being open late, it was frequented by lorry drivers and young guys with motorbikes or scooters. Eddie, the owner, a refugee from alcoholism and the Earl's Court scene, was gay, and so were some of the customers—leatherboys, skinheads, and even a few locals.

Monday nights were usually very quiet at the Roundhouse and this one was no exception. I chatted with Eddie and a pair of leatherboys I knew, and after less than an hour, decided to head back down the Holloway Road to Tollington Way and home.

Halfway there, I saw him coming toward me. There was no doubt it was Harry Telford, and as soon as he saw me, he ran forward, shouting my name. "Did you think I'd forgotten you?"

"Well, yes!"

"Sorry. I've been working all hours. Got a few days off now." He turned around and walked beside me.

And then I noticed. He was wearing a striped, knitted pullover and tweed cap, almost identical to the cover boy's outfit on the front of *A Boy's Book of Wonders*. My blended image of Harry and the imaginary boy from the 1920's had suddenly manifested in front of me.

"Like your jumper!" I said.

"I never wear it, it's a bit scratchy. Don't know why I put it on today."

I threw my arm around his shoulder and we walked quietly along together.

Harry had the bright, inquisitive eyes and boyish looks that I always found attractive, though I liked talkative people, and Harry seldom spoke, and then in brief outbursts punctuated with long stretches of silence.

Glad as I was to see him, I suddenly felt enormously tired. We arranged to meet at Sarge's shop the next evening. Harry caught a bus, and I finished my walk home alone, crashed into bed and quickly fell off to sleep.

Waiting for Harry after work the next day, I told Sarge what had happened. He finished rolling his cigarette, gave a little laugh, and looked out the window.

"There's only one Mind," he said. "The one we're using now!"

And he blew a smoke ring that rose very slowly above his head, and hovered above him for a moment, like a tilted halo.

Harry showed up right on time. As it happened, he turned out to be a chronic fibber with far too many problems. And his sister wasn't really his sister. But that's another story. We did have some good times together. And for a long while I kept the tweed cap he left one night in my room and never did come back for.

SOAKERS AND SCAVENGERS

Soon after I moved to the Finsbury Park district of London in the early 1980s, I discovered Boris Mostoyenko's stamp shop, which also served as a convenient hangout for various local lads. The front part of Boris's store was usually taken up with used furniture, machines in various states of disrepair, and all manner of scavenged items that Boris and Sarge (who ran a military surplus outlet a couple of streets away) found, bought, sold, gave away, and traded through a network of scrap dealers, old furniture merchants, rubbish tip managers, Oxfam shops, and private garages. Much of the material had been discarded. An aisle through the middle of this dubious treasure trove led to a set of handsome glass-topped wooden counters in dark wood spanning the width of the shop—salvaged, Boris said, from an old hardware store. In front of them were several wooden stools.

Under the glass of the counter were displayed various stamp sets and packets, plus occasional odd items like cigarette cards, matchbook labels, beer coasters, and stick-on political slogans (Boris favored "Don't Vote—It Only Encourages Them!" and "No Matter Who You Vote For—the Government Always Gets In!"). There was also a selection of political and religious pamphlets, most of them in foreign languages. Behind the serving area, tall, matching cabinets with brass-handled drawers held long boxes of foreign stamps. In the middle of the drawers an opening led to a large back room where a big round wooden table was surrounded by assorted, mismatched chairs. There was a couch, long enough for a tall lad to sleep on. This was Boris's kitchen. A back door led to a tiny, untended back lot and a small rundown outbuilding.

Here, Boris could be found from about midday until bedtime. (He was a notoriously late riser and used to say he could deal with anything as long as he didn't have to get up in the morning.) Boris was a wiry, middle-aged bloke of medium height and military bearing, balding, with rimless spectacles, a wry manner and a quiet way of keeping the otherwise unruly in reasonably good order, like a good schoolteacher. He spoke good English with just a trace of an indefinable accent. He was of mixed Russian, Belorussian, Ukrainian, and Polish background—"a proud European mongrel. Not Mongol, *mongrel!*" He had fled Central Europe at the end of the War, coming to England via Vienna and Liechtenstein. When not looking after the shop, he could usually be found washing up at the sink, a hand-rolled cigarette dangling from his lip.

Stamp customers were welcome in the shop until six when the OPEN sign on the front door was turned to CLOSED. After that, entry was by invitation only. Boris's warm kitchen and big table provided a refuge from bad weather, boredom, and for some of us, the squalor of squatters' quarters. Regulars included Elliot and Lionel, a teenaged pair known as the Triplets, who lived upstairs with Boris, several local lads including my skinhead friends Andy and Paul, and (on Saturdays) the philatelic supplies salesman Windom Price, tall, campy and very funny, who ran the perennially struggling *Hampstead and Highgate Shoppers News* with his elderly mother. Windom could be relied upon to bring us our fortnightly copy of *Gay News* which Boris and I both eagerly devoured and which always made the Triplets shriek with laughter. (A picture of Cliff Richard, taken from an early issue, had adorned Boris's notice board for years. The Triplets' love-hate attitude to Cliff Richard was among the most minor of their small eccentricities.)

From the beginning, I was made welcome at the shop. As a stamp collector since my Uncle Sid had given me a big cigar box full of duplicates many years before, I had learned something about philately. This meant that I could *sort—without supervision!—*and like everyone else at Boris's, I was soon put to work, paying with casual labor for my free tea and cheap sandwiches. For, as I soon learned, Boris's place was not just a "leisure centre for lay-abouts" as the local tobacconist described it, but the hub of an extensive, cobbled-together philatelic system.

Foreign stamps—used ones, at any rate—seldom just appear on the dealer's doorstep. They have to be scavenged—from foreign mail and, in the case of revenues, from documents of various sorts. I soon found that acquiring these in large numbers was Boris's forte.

"Boris's shop was the hub of
an extensive, cobbled-together philatelic system."

London business relied in those days on a seemingly vast number of messengers to keep its communications and deliveries going. Smartly dressed couriers in blazers and rolled umbrellas, uniformed commissionaires, young blokes on bikes dashing through the winding, traffic-clogged streets at a hair-raising pace, and a mid-sized army of inconspicuous foot messengers, many of whom were Middle-European men of a certain age, crisscrossed the city with packets, envelopes, and documents about their persons. These men (there were apparently no women) all seemed to know Boris and constituted the front rank of his army of stamp scavengers.

Boris explained that several of the outfits employing these men were reliable old London firms of high reputation. Others, he said, seemed to be "run out of an old boot." Nonetheless, their various contacts in banks, offices, government agencies, and missions gave their employees, Boris's confederates, access to numerous foreign stamps, all of which were duly scavenged, saved in plastic bags, and picked up by Boris's couriers (usually Elliot, Lionel, Andy, Paul or occasionally myself) and delivered to Boris every few days.

I soon got to know many of Boris's scavengers and heard bits of their often intriguing histories. It seemed almost standard practice for scavengers to represent (or claim to represent) various political organizations in exile, ethnic benevolent societies, quasi-military social clubs or obscure religious denominations. The Galician Social Center, the Macedonian Independence League and (a favorite of Boris's) the Chapel of St. Sergius and St. Bacchus were only a few among the many. My own favorite title was held by the voluble, but always exhausted-looking Henry Wilson (originally Henryk Vishnitzkiy), Acting Secretary of the Workers Party of Western Ukraine (Menshevik Caucus). I never dared ask him how many members this organization had but I can't imagine the meetings got very crowded.

Petru Cretzulescu, a voluble little man with a limp, was an officer (probably the only officer) of the Romanian Social Democratic Party in exile. For years he had been assembling a manuscript entitled *Laugh? I Nearly Died! A Buried Treasury of Concentration Camp Humour.* Arne Minko, who ran the Cross-Channel Messenger Service, was a dapper, pleasant-looking man with a small Chancellor Dollfuss mustache, a vaguely naval get-up and an unidentifiable accent. He always brought high-value revenues, sometimes on discarded documents. Minko was himself a stamp collector, specializing in a number of out-of-the-way places like Lundy Island, Fiume, and Central Lithuania.

LONDON SKIN & BONES

Sandor Poganyi had avoided persecution by the Hungarian communists by the simple expedient of getting himself confined to a lunatic asylum, where he stayed until the brief revolution of 1956 allowed him to flee the country. Sandor, who had fiery red hair and protruding, goiterous eyes, wrote long poems in Hungarian and lamented the loss of his former boyfriend ("my great romance") whom he had first met by communicating through toilet pipes in the asylum (they were housed on different floors). Sandor was always trying to get someone to translate his poems but as they were a) very long and b) written, I was told, in rather flowery, antiquated Hungarian, he had no luck.

For the most part, the scavengers came in one at a time, usually bustling through on the way to deliver an envelope or small parcel. Occasionally, one of them would linger and then, almost inevitably it seemed, another would quickly appear at the door. Within minutes we would be in the middle of a lively discussion between a Jewish syndicalist from Swiss Cottage and a Polish monarchist from Highgate Hill over the difference between Ruthenia and the Carpatho-Ukraine, which apparently was a big deal in certain circles.

Walter Linder was another regular, an Austrian expatriate whose unusual story he told me as we were devouring a couple of Boris's sandwiches (which were invariably of two varieties—corned beef and Branston pickle, cheese and beetroot). Linder was well into his sixties by the time I met him, and semi-retired from his job in a City bank. He still came in occasionally to drop off stamps. He had been a young man in Vienna when the German Anschluss came in 1937.

"My family was not Jewish, thank God," he explained, "but my father was a socialist and we wanted to get out quickly. Father had become fairly well-off and had amassed a stamp collection that was unique with many arcane and unusual items. Officially, it was owned by my father's company for tax reasons. Now something you may not know"—he looked over to Boris who nodded silently as Walter continued—"is that Ernst Kaltenbrunner, one of the top Nazi big shots, a real monster, was an avid stamp collector! And my father's stamp collection turned out to be our ace in the hole. Kaltenbrunner knew about it as he knew about a lot of things, and he coveted it. I had banking powers for my father's company—not that there was much left of it—and access to the safe where the stamp collection was kept. Through an intermediary, I offered the collection to Kaltenbrunner in return for safe passage out of Austria for my parents and my sister and myself. And, surprisingly easily, the deal was done. We were out and the bank turned over the collection as instructed.

"My father could never decide whether to be happy I saved their lives or to be angry with me for losing his stamp collection: 'Those Sikkimese revenues were among the finest forgeries ever printed,' he grumbled to me more than once. I don't suppose Kaltenbrunner ever knew his prize Sikkimese revenues were forgeries. He was hanged, as you know, and the collection—more of an accumulation really—was broken up and sold. I've seen items from it on the market, including a copy of the Bohemia & Moravia Heydrich Death Mask souvenir sheet in a sinister-looking black leather folder with Kaltenbrunner's signature scrawled across Heydrich's face. Twice I've even seen some of the Sikkimese revenues—both times offered as genuine."

"You didn't say anything?" I asked.

"Believe me," he answered with a little smile, "it's not of the slightest consequence."

Walter and I had been chatting at Boris's table, and Boris chimed in while consulting a catalogue. "I met a soldier once, an American, we had quite a nice time together," he confided. "He had been a guard at Spandau for a while, after the War. So he had seen Kaltenbrunner close up. Not a pleasant sight, he told me. He was rather a freak, almost seven feet tall with a huge head, massive shoulders, and a glowering, deeply lined face disfigured by duelling scars. My friend said he had very long, hairy arms and small, womanish hands. Very creepy." And Boris headed into the shop to attend to a customer.

There were also people—friends, neighbors, and others—who saved stamps from their own post and passed them on to Boris. Mrs. Singh, who ran the local laundrette, carefully saved the occasional interesting stamp from her husband's veterinary practice. Most of the stamps that regularly came into the shop in this way remained attached to their ragged envelope corners or cut-square pieces of document. Some, I noticed, stayed attached to their "covers," and these Boris especially prized. A fine envelope, beautifully printed, from some swanky bank with finely franked foreign stamps could send Boris into one of his small ecstasies; you could always tell because he would crack a crinkly little smile and look at the ceiling. If a cache was especially good, he would silently cross himself.

The next necessary step in the process was the soaking, and this Boris had organized with amiable efficiency. In houses and flats all over North-East London, Boris's soakers supplemented their incomes by floating stamps off bits of envelope and drying them between sheets of blotting paper. Here the ladies came into their own. The sisters Edna and Vera Williams, old friends of Boris who ran a wool and knitwear shop in Wanstead High Street, were among the regulars, as were several shut-ins and semi-invalids. By far the most prolific soaker was Aunt Doll, a plump, talkative old thing with a liking for bright turban-like headgear, amber pendants, and big brooches, a dressmaker who ran a corner shop just outside Chipping Ongar. A small cellar room of her cottage was stacked with plastic trays for water and large sheets of blotting paper on shallow shelves—a veritable philatelic production line.

A bit of soaking even went on at Boris's, mostly as something for Orbit to do. Orbit was a good-natured but rather dim lad of about twenty with bright, multi-colored hair, blubbery lips, blotchy skin, and a lazy eye. He was an enthusiastic soaker, floating and drying with the best of them, his enthusiasm often accompanied by a slight side-to-side rocking motion and a series of low, rhythmic sounds rather like gutteral humming.

The soakers having finished their work, the stamps, dried and free of adhesions, were bagged and returned to Boris, where they were added to other lots purchased in bulk and set before whoever happened to be sitting at the round table, ready for the essential next step—sorting. Whichever two or three of us happened to be warming ourselves in Boris's kitchen, drinking his tea, would be pressed into service sorting mixed bags of stamps into country lots. Skinhead carpet-layers and squatters on the dole soon learned that Magyar Kir Posta meant Hungary and Shqiperia meant Albania. The more dedicated prided themselves in being able to tell Kiauchau from Kouang-Cheou, Congo (Brazzaville) from Congo (Leopoldville), Somalia from Somaliland, and Inhambane from Quelimane ...

Sorted thus into countries, the stamps were looted quickly by Boris for his renowned packets (TEN TANNU TOUVA, TWENTY-FIVE TRIANGLES & DIAMONDS, TWENTY BOXING & FENCING). The remainder were stuffed into glassine envelopes, ready for the most tedious stage of the process—careful identification by number and catalogue value from the pages of Stanley Gibbons. Requiring a certain meticulousness, many stamps being similar to one another, perhaps differing only by shade or perforation variety, this stage allowed me to make what was undoubtedly my greatest contribution to Boris's shop—introducing him (over the phone—I don't believe they ever met) to my old school friend Laurie Andrews. Laurie's semi-reclusive nature and love of minutiae and routine made him ideally suited to the task of cataloguing, but by far his most valuable asset was his retentive, near-photographic memory. Once he had identified the catalogue number and value of a particular stamp, he never forgot it. He became an invaluable part of Boris's team. Every month I would visit Laurie on Friday with a box of glassines from Boris, and return on Monday with last month's numbered cards ready for pricing. Boris never ceased to be amazed and delighted at Laurie's uncanny talent.

Boris's shop, tucked away in a grimy, impoverished part of London, provided not only free tea and a warm, congenial place to hang out, but occupation, income, and something of an education in political geography for his diverse array of soakers, scavengers and sorters. His sandwiches, though predictable, were always fresh. The tea was free. And Aunt Doll? Every so often someone would ask, "Whose aunt *is* she anyway?"

"Everybody's."

THE BUGGERY CLUB

The Finsbury Park Men's & Boys' Boxing Club was housed in a crumbling brick warehouse off the Holloway Road. It had been a significant club as late as the 1960s. By the '80s it seemed perpetually on its last legs but stubbornly refused to go down for the count and provided a center of social as well as athletic activity for a selection of local lads. Andy Boom and one or two of his pals had taken to sparring there and Tommy Noakes, a burly journeyman middleweight, made it his home base. I was standing outside the club with Andy and Tommy on an overcast Friday afternoon.

"I'm not sure I like the look of those eyebrows," Tommy was complaining; he was talking about Andy's friend Paul Tyler. The two skinheads had taken up amateur boxing at the suggestion of the Old Sarge. It seemed to do them good, channeling a worrisome capacity for violence into what Tommy called "good healthy pummelling." I was grateful to Sarge, Tommy, and the club manager Seamus Moore for giving Andy's penchant for brawling a legitimate outlet; I badly wanted him to stay out of jail.

My Dad had done a bit of amateur boxing in his Air Force days and I'd picked up an interest from sitting with him as a kid in Canada, watching the Gillette Friday Night Fights on TV and listening to his commentary. For me though, boxing was strictly a spectator sport. I'm a runner, not a fighter.

"Young Paul can punch all right, that right hook—that right hook comes natural to him," said Tommy. "Fast too. Tall. Good reach. Nice left jab." He darted little glances at Andy and me, and was obviously brooding about something.

"*But ... ?*" I asked.

"Well, he's very strong, see."

I looked surprised at Tommy seeming to see Paul's strength as a liability.

"He's not a very big boy. He's stronger than his frame can handle. Might be a bit prone to injury. And," Tommy added, "I'm not sure I like the look of those eyebrows. He might get cut a lot."

Andy grinned. "Wouldn't want him bleeding all over our nice clean ring, would we!"

"But he's a good boy, good amateur," Tommy was quick to admit. "He'll do himself credit ... You got that *Gay News?*" Andy handed it over.

Before Andy and Paul started showing up at the club, Tommy and the irascible Seamus Moore were the only openly gay members, though we had our suspicions (or more than suspicions) about a few of the regulars. "He may be on the straight and narrow now," said Tommy about one handsome heavyweight, "but I think he's been 'round the corner ... Well, I *know* he's been 'round the corner. And he's had a look! He's had a *good* look!"

"Anything on tonight, Tommy?" asked Andy.

"I want to go to this new Buggery Club," Tommy blurted out, causing me and Andy to chirp up, almost in unison, "This *what?*"

"*The.* Listen to me. *Buggery.* Are you listening? *Club.* Didn't anyone tell you about it? Some skins have got a place in some back street in Camden. They're running booze and music there on the weekends. Some of the boys get a bit wild, I hear."

"Is it licenced?" I asked stupidly.

"Shouldn't think so," Tommy said. "They've got beer though. Thought we'd have a look for it tonight. A mate of mine told me where it is more or less. Come with us, we'll all have a go."

"It's not boneheads is it?" I had no interest in getting involved with the neo-Nazi skins we called boneheads, but Tommy assured me these lads were strictly a gay or gay-friendly lot. "I said buggery, darlin', not thuggery!"

The press tended to depict all skinheads as right-wing hooligans but while some more than fitted the bill, we dismissed the stereotype as just a way to sell newspapers, fads and fashions generally being more subtle than they seem. The Park skins I knew were far from the neo-Nazis of popular mythology. Most of them were non-political or vaguely Labourite, and Andy and Paul were part of our "armchair anarchist" contingent headquartered around the big table at the back of Boris Mostoyenko's stamp shop.

LONDON SKIN & BONES

In the early 80s, the Punk movement was in full swing with an array of bizarre, colorful hairstyles and ripped clothes held together with safety pins. The Punks around Finsbury Park were outrageous ragamuffins, mostly squatters, or on the dole—lifestyles the skins disdained, seeing themselves as clean, patriotic working class blokes. Skins were proud, clean-shaven roundheads rather than tatty cavaliers; they cut their hair almost to the skull, wore Doc Martens work boots, tight jeans or Sta-Press trousers held up with braces ("suspenders" in American translation), plain shirts or T-shirts and Crombie overcoats. They reminded me of Hutterites minus the beards and hats. Their simple style was basically that of young manual workers with a dash of Mod flair. I found it very sexy—and Andy and I agreed the Buggery Club sounded like an irresistible prospect for a Friday night out.

We all arranged to meet at the Black Cap pub in Camden at 10 o'clock that night. I was the last to arrive and found the lads in conference with one of the locals—a regular customer at Boris's. Brian Bevis was an eccentric, good-natured gent of sixty or so, an ex-Army intelligence officer who always introduced himself as "Brian Bevis, Anarcho-Monarchist!" He had a calling card printed up bearing that inscription and an emblem he'd designed—the anarchist A in a circle—topped with a crown. Brian claimed to be a member of an obscure group founded in Spain whose most prominent member (what am I saying—whose *only* prominent member) was the painter Salvador Dalí.

Brian was a tall, aristocratic looking man with a thick mane of immaculately coiffed silver hair; he always wore a blazer and the old boys' tie of one of the more obscure Public Schools. He had (Sarge had assured me) served with distinction in the post-war Malayan campaign where he had lost his left arm and left eye in a munitions explosion. One blazer sleeve tucked into a pocket took care of the missing arm; the eye had been replaced by a glass one, over which he habitually wore a monocle. At Boris's once, Brian explained that he did this on the premise that people would notice the monocle and overlook the staring glass eye. I couldn't decide whether this was logical or not, but as I said, Brian was eccentric. And he had, he readily confessed, "an eye for the boys—*this* one! I can't get the glass one to see a thing! Must get this monocle seen to!" He laughed at his own much repeated joke.

By the time I came in the doors of the Black Cap, it had already been decided that Brian would be our guide to the night's destination, the so-

47

called Buggery Club, located in a back street down by the canal, which after a cursory glance at Tommy's handmade map, Brian assured us he could find, no trouble at all. He was holding forth quite loudly as I sat down.

"I was just telling these chaps," (he lowered his voice a few decibels) "about the parliamentary debates we had about legalizing queers back in the Sixties. I expect you were a bit young then, weren't you. What a frightful row that was! The bill was sponsored in the Lords by old Boofy Arran, who kept a tame badger in his house. I met him once, smelled a bit—the badger not Boofy who was a very clean old man. And in the commons our champion was a Mr. Abse, a Welsh Jew I think, who wore op art waistcoats."

"Did these things help?" asked Tommy, "or put people off?"

"I don't think anyone paid much attention," Brian ruminated. "But some of the old fogeys were blue in the face over the prospect of making us legal. Monty—Lord Montgomery of Alamein Right, who did so well against Rommel—thundered that we were about to 'condone the Devil and all his works.'"

Andy let out a whoop.

"'*We* are not *French!*' Monty shouted at the assembled House of Lords. 'We are Englishmen, thank God!'"

Andy and Paul thumped on the table at this.

"Another old fart warned that legalizing us would result in 'an immediate rush on the part of tutors and army officers'—I liked that one—'into acts of mass buggery!'"

Brian continued these fond reminiscences as we finished our drinks.

"The British people were warned, you see, that legalizing us would mean the establishment of 'buggery clubs' all over England, and in Wales too, I suppose. *Buggery clubs!* Well, as you can imagine, I could hardly wait. Alas! Well, apart from some very nice, rather well-mannered establishments, it never happened. *Until now!* All these years later!

"Of course," he said with a shrug, "legalization hit the aristocracy very hard. At least one old country squire was convinced it meant the end of everything he held dear, or else he got frightened he could no longer resist temptation. Went up into his study, opened up the Game Book—you know, big ledger where you write up whatever birds and animals you've shot that day on the estate—wrote his own name in it—and blew his head off. Now I'd say that was taking punctilio to an extreme!"

"Well, come on Brian, drink up," urged Paul. "Show us the way!" And

LONDON SKIN & BONES

the five of us headed out into Camden Town. The evening was getting cool and Tommy said he thought it might rain.

We ended up in a little lane beside the Camden Lock, bordered by warehouses and decaying old brick lockups. Tommy and Brian were scrutinizing the map while Andy and Paul and I stood by the side of the canal gossiping about our friend Boris and the two teenage brothers who lived with him.

"You ever been upstairs at Boris's?" Paul asked.

"Yes!" said I. "It's like a museum up there, all sorts of old clutter. Mostly the Triplets' stuff, closets full of clothes, lots of costumes, cowboy and Indian gear and theater props and old masks, some nice sex toys. Hatboxes full of feathers. What with them and Boris's candlesticks and religious bits and pieces and all the furniture, there's quite a hoard."

"The Triplets came home with me once," Paul confided. "Quite fun but they love to play all these odd games. I suppose that's why they like Boris so much. He acts out all their stories with them and hides under the blankets while they tickle each other with feathers and whisper word games. Boris doesn't mind it all, he quite gets into the spirit of it. I think it's all a bit much for me but I did have fun. They tied me up at one point and painted their faces with shaving soap."

"I wonder what either one of them would be like on his own," said Andy.

"I think they're strictly a double act," I said. "If you're with one, the other's watching."

"Am I the only one who hasn't had sex with Elliot and Lionel?" Andy asked.

"There's still time," said Paul. "Maybe we could double date."

"I'm not much for theatrical performances," admitted Andy. He thought for a moment. "*Although* ..."

Suddenly we heard Tommy alerting us to a door opening some distance down the lane. A few likely lads were emerging from one of the warehouses.

"There it is, come on," said Brian, and strode on ahead of us, swinging his single arm.

A pair of skinheads were horsing around as we got to the green metal door of the old building. The doorkeeper was a fellow about my age, mid-thirties.

"Squaddie!" Tommy knew him by name.

"Tommy! Lookin' for a fight?" Squaddie wore a peaked forage cap, American camouflage fatigues, and polished boots. Lean, handsome, and clean-shaven with a square jaw, he reminded me of the space pilot Dan Dare in the old *Eagle* comics I devoured as a boy.

"I'm off duty, darlin'," Tommy answered.

As the door opened, the heavy beat of a band leaked into the laneway.

"Who's playing?" Andy asked.

"TBH." I'd heard this lot before. TBH was a Camden group—a juicy mix of black skinheads and white Rastas. Their music was a mix of reggae and old pub and music hall chestnuts delivered with a raw, punky sound and rudimentary instrumentals. Their signature tune was a raucous, reggae version of the wartime Vera Lynn anthem "We'll Meet Again."

As Tommy and Squaddie bantered, I noticed Squaddie eyeing Brian Bevis. A sixty-year old man with one arm and a monocle, wearing a blazer and highly polished oxfords, was hardly an expected guest at the Camden boys' Buggery Club. But before Tommy could vouch for us all, Brian included, a nearby commotion caused Squaddie to leave his place at the door and march around the corner to see what was happening. He sent a couple of noisy lads on their way and rejoined us.

"Don't want to upset the neighbors!"

Brian's eye had fallen upon Squaddie. "Brian Bevis, Anarcho-Monarchist!" he boomed, extending his one big hand in Squaddie's direction.

Squaddie took Brian's hand in his with a quizzical look.

"Green Jacket, were you?" Brian asked.

"I *was*!" said Squaddie, taken by surprise. "How did you know?"

"Rifle Brigade!" Brian barked. "Always recognize that quick march!"

Brian and Squaddie, it seems, had been in similar army units in different decades and now it was Old Soldiers' Night all over the place as the two of them stood about swapping stories. The rest of us were waved in.

I was never much of a clubber. I drink hardly at all and don't take chemicals or dance all night. But like every other gay fellow in London, I turned up at some of the clubs now and then. My favorite was the Catacombe Club in Earl's Court (Seamus Moore called it the Catamite Club). Always packed, it was a cozy underground hideaway with a bar, a dance floor, and a series of alcoves with booths in them where you could sit quite comfortably with friends old and new. A beautiful, long-haired Hawaiian boy called Keoni used to dance there with his Canadian lover, and on occasion the MP Tom Driberg would show up with a small entourage.

Another rendezvous was the Carousel Club, hidden down one of the twisting lanes adjoining Soho. The Carousel, up two flights of stairs, had acquired several seats for two from old roundabouts ,and these were arranged around walls painted with fairground and circus images. An old trompe-l'œil mural of the London skyline at night (said to be by Rex Whistler) surrounded french doors leading to a small roof garden with a few metal tables and chairs crammed onto it and benches around the outside—most welcome on hot nights.

The West End club Heaven and its new rival, Hell ("Going to Heaven tonight?" "No, I'm going to Hell!") were more upscale, and more expensive, with admission fees which our crowd couldn't afford. But you could get into Heaven for nothing if you went on Uniform Nights. The drill was to go before ten o'clock and say you were there for the Uniform Club. No actual uniform was required, and once in, you could stay as long as you wanted. But all these clubs were a long way from Finsbury Park and, London Transport being what it was, entailed a long trip home by bus and on foot at the end of the night. The Buggery Club was closer to home.

The back door opened onto a big room with a high ceiling, probably once part of a warehouse. Raised platforms served as a stage and DJ booth, round metal tables and plastic chairs were arrayed around the walls and bottles or cold beer were served out of oil drums. There was a cramped, fetid bathroom and a haze of pot and tobacco smoke.

The Buggery Club soon filled up with skinheads, punks, and other lads. TBH filled the place with sound. Then came records from the turntable as the boys took a break and mixed with the mob. No actual buggery could be detected but the night was young. As the place grew hot and stifling, I fled for a while to the cool damp of the laneway. A breeze was springing up and it felt as though a storm was in the offing. I stood in the darkness by the canal; every time the door opened, there was a blast of sound from the records—the Police's "Don't Stand So Close to Me," the Boomtown Rats' "I Don't Like Mondays," the Clash's "London Calling."

After a while I plunged back into the fray, catching up with Andy having a drink with a curly-headed young fellow we'd noticed earlier. "This is Mitch!" Hello's all round; Mitch seemed very friendly. Andy went off to get another beer and left me and Mitch in the crush discussing the relative merits of Blondie and Queen, shouted over the din, which meant we got up close and personal.

TBH started up again, bold and loud. Their lead singer was a skinny white lad with tattoos, dreadlocks, and a fashionable sneer. They launched into their trademark shouted, spittle-flecked take on the hoary old urban folk songs of our cockney forefathers:

"Mother Brown said Darlin'
You've got a nasty cough.
If I catch you bending,
I'll saw your legs right off!

O! Knees up Mother Brown,
Knees up Mother Brown!
Ee-eye ee-eye ee-eye O!
Under the table she must go!

Knees up! Knees up!
Never get the breeze up!
Knees up Mother Brown!
Oi!"

The heat, the noise, the people—I was getting ready to flee when Andy and Mitch came up, arms around one another, suggesting we all go back to Turle Road for the night. Mitch was a freckle-faced lad with tight trousers, a ready smile, and bright eyes behind thick, plastic-rimmed glasses. I was ready to go. TBH finished their spirited rendition of "My Old Man's a Dustman! / He wears a dustman's hat! / He wears cor blimey trousers! / What do you think o'that?" And soon Tommy and Paul were in the middle of a line that was swaying drunkenly to "The Lambeth Walk," Tommy with a beer bottle tucked in his belt. I wondered, could "Hands, knees, and boomps a'daisy!" be far behind? The skins were sweating and jumping about, and the decibel level was now approaching deafening.

"Where's the Beast with Five Fingers?" shouted Andy.

"Brian? He's over there!"

As we headed out the door, we passed Brian sitting with Squaddie at a

LONDON SKIN & BONES

table full of beer bottles, his one meaty hand on Squaddie's thigh, shouting in his ear "You're a fine figure of a man, Squaddie!"

"What?"

"A fine figure of a man!"

Squaddie had his eyes closed and a big grin on his face. Brian was as red as a radish. We signaled with hand gestures as we passed them, heading for the door. A chalkboard with a scrawled notice announced:

NEXT WEEK
ROMFORD
ROOD BOYS

Brian waved us through as he and Squaddie broke into a chorus of "Sod 'em all! Sod 'em all! / The long and the short and the tall ... / There'll be some pro-*motion* this side of the *ocean* ..."

By this point, the cacophony, the smoke, and the heat had become overwhelming, and the damp night air outside was a welcome relief. The three of us walked a few yards to the canal. While the others mopped their faces with handkerchiefs, I leaned against a tree and stared at the black water. An extensive old canal and lock system had once wound through much of London. Now only Camden Lock, a picturesque stretch by Regents Park, and a few other fragments remained. As I was musing what it must have been like in its heyday, someone closed a nearby window with a loud bang. It occurred to me that the Buggery Club, even if it did try not to annoy the neighbors, might not be around for long.

A sudden cool gust of wind swept by and I turned up the collar of my coat. Andy came over to me and put his arm around my shoulder.

"Ready to go?"

Before I could answer, the heavens opened and the long-awaited deluge rained down with a vengeance.

As I huddled with Andy and Mitch in a nearby doorway, we quickly decided to head for Mitch's place only a couple of streets away, rather than make the long journey in the rain back to Finsbury Park.

The three of us hurried down the road with newspapers over our heads.

'Where do you live?" Andy asked.

"Up by Hawley Road," Mitch answered. "I live with Squaddie."

"Squaddie won't mind you bringing two blokes home?"

"No," Mitch laughed. "He likes you!"

Andy and I shot each other a glance but we were in for a Pound now and the rain was falling hard. We got to the corner and looked back toward the club, only to see Squaddie and Brian, holding each other up, singing "The Rifles, the Skins and the Bold Fusiliers." They were following a bit unsteadily in our footsteps, undoubtedly heading to the same place we were.

Suddenly the sky lit up with a magnificent streak of lightning, followed by a loud crack of nearby thunder. Everyone started to run, laughing and shouting.

Oh well, I thought, what the hell. Wet or dry, one way or another, I'd say we're in for a long night.

THE MAN
WHO SHOT PEABODY DREDD

I only saw Peabody Dredd once. I was in the Boltons, a leather bar in Earl's Court, and there he was, perched on a bar stool talking to someone. Not that we were ever introduced but it could only have been him. A tall, muscular black man with flashing eyes, dreadlocks, and a brutal scar across one eye, disfiguring his nose. He was wearing a tight, white T-shirt and army fatigues with a special pocket for his flashlight. I wandered round the pub, didn't see anyone I fancied, and left for the Colhearne along the street.

Of course, I had heard the name Peabody Dredd in and around Finsbury Park where he was said to have been a resident of Michael de Freitas's "Black House" around 1970. De Frietas had been a pimp, a petty criminal, and an enforcer for the slumlord Peter Rachman. When Black Power suddenly became all the rage, de Freitas decided to cash in. He began calling himself Michael X and conned John Lennon into funding the "revolutionary Black Power commune" he started on the Holloway Road. Then he got involved in a bank robbery but was allowed to flee the country when he threatened to send obscene photos of Princess Margaret to the tabloids. He went back to his native Trinidad where he was eventually hanged for murder.

Peabody's part in the Black House escapade was never clear but even so, his imposing stature and heavily-scarred face tended to make most people give him a wide berth. It turned out he had close connections with a few people I knew in the district they called The Park. I learned about that in the most unlikely of places—at a slightly drunken but otherwise very civilized garden party just outside Chipping Ongar in the far leafy suburbs of North-East London.

I had known the Andrews family for several years. My Uncle Fred had worked with Poddy Andrews when they were editors together at ITV. Poddy was an easygoing, gray-haired, middle-class bourgeois bohemian. His wife Jean, who made jewelry, had been a great beauty in her day; she was pretty and funny and loved to fuss over young male visitors. Poddy and Jean lived in a rambling stone cottage "on the cutting edge of Chipping Ongar" as Poddy liked to say, with two of their three handsome children. Catherine, one of those quintessentially breezy English girls with rosy cheeks, a quick smile and a liking for long, diaphanous flower print dresses, had married her college tutor and moved to Oxford. Robert, the youngest, was usually away at college. It was Laurie, the sweet-natured but eccentric middle child, whom I had become friends with. As he was nervous and uneasy with the world outside the neighborhood, Laurie seldom ventured far from home, his life revolving around a routine of circumscribed activities, one of which was entertaining me on regular monthly visits. On these occasions, we would go for walks in the nearby woods, repeat, with small variations his favorite bondage games, and share our avid mutual interest in stamp collecting.

Poddy and Jean loved to have parties, and sometimes held them to coincide with one of my visits. It was on one of these happy occasions, which usually spilled out into their large back garden, that I heard a fair portion of the story of the man who shot Peabody Dredd.

I had brought with me as my guest Mr. Seamus Moore, unofficial Poet Laureate of the Laundrettes. Seamus was a tall, big-boned man with a raw, grizzled face; he was wearing a cable-knit pullover and sandals and held an almost empty wine glass. "Have to come round for tea and biscuits," he liked to urge me. "I've got some lovely books to show you and we'll light up a smoke or two." Seamus lived near me in Finsbury Park and shared my liking for cannabis and modern literature. It was a deliciously warm night and as we stood together in the garden, the fragrance of the flowers Poddy and Jean took such good care of wafted toward us on the evening breeze. A couple of little groups of guests stood or sat here and there and through the French doors I could see Laurie playing the piano and his brother Robert—so similar in looks and different in temperament—pretending to conduct an imaginary orchestra. People stood about in small groups with glasses in their hands.

As we talked, Poddy came toward us with tea for Seamus, served—wisely, I thought—in an enamel mug as Seamus, who greatly enjoyed a drink, had become a bit wobbly on his feet. I was glad that our friend Rose had her car on hand to drive him home.

"Ah!" exclaimed Seamus. "Tea for the dragon!" Poddy handed him the mug and he took a sip. *"Bread for the birds!"* he shouted, taking some crusts from the feeding table and scattering them on the lawn. *"And wine for the gods!"* He threw the dregs of his wine onto the lawn after them.

"Would you mind?" asked Poddy with a wink, "if I take Seamus away for a few moments? There's someone I want him to meet." And the two of them headed back into the house, Seamus with his arm around Poddy's neck and his big hand on Poddy's shoulder. They had only just met but were already acting like lifelong friends.

As Poddy and Seamus helped each other into the house, I turned my attention to a thin, middle-aged woman sitting on a nearby bench smoking a cigarette. She was dressed in a tweed skirt, a powder blue cardigan with a string of large, purple beads, and white canvas plimsolls.

"Hello Susan."

"Hello dear, haven't seen you in an age," she acknowledged, blowing a smoke ring in the direction of the hollyhocks.

Susan Peskett was the older sister of an acquaintance—never a friend—of about a decade, the eccentric Nigel Peskett, a notorious political troublemaker. I had first encountered Nigel in the very early Seventies at meetings of the newly formed Gay Liberation Front, held in an old church. The large gatherings were made up mostly of young people—students, workers, squatters—and discussions in the big hall were lively, vocal, and sometimes raucous, with some people showing up in then-fashionable semi-drag. Almost everyone was allowed his or her say, but a few people eventually had to be gently excluded. One of them was Nigel, who in those days was a skinny youth, spotty, pasty-faced, and oddly dressed. Nigel was one of a small minority who wanted GLF to ally itself with a radical group of pompous, self-styled urban terrorists called the Angry Brigade. Young Nigel became a one-man angry brigade of his own, demanding immediate revolutionary action to overthrow monarchy, parliament and bourgeois standards of behavior, and making such a nuisance of himself that he was soon advised to move on. For a while he took up an ersatz occultism which involved filing his front teeth to points in the belief that he was imitating Aleister Crowley. He then faded from view.

In the late Seventies, the fragmentation of an ultra-right-wing political party called the National Front threw up a number of small splinter groups, one of which was the British Party, which enjoyed small pockets of mostly youthful support in two or three London districts, including Finsbury Park. Its unlikely leader was none other than a radically made-over Nigel Peskett. Though he had gotten rid of the spots, the new Nigel was just as pasty-faced as the old one but a considerable weight gain had transformed the once rail-thin youth into a pudgy, freely perspiring young man. The frocks and fatigues had been replaced by flannels and blazers. His oily hair was beginning to thin, and his alarmingly pointed teeth had become mere disfigured—and discolored—stumps. Instead of calling for class warfare or muttering about the black arts, he now preached a half-baked crypto-fascism whose main talking points were restoring the British Empire and suggesting to colored immigrants that they might like to go back where they came from.

I had never spoken to Nigel in his previous incarnation as a GLF hanger-on but I had run into the new, fatter, more right-wing Nigel a few months earlier at a demo against council house rent increases. Nigel's little group had been skulking around the edges of the crowd and as the demo broke up, Yob, one of our lads, who obviously knew him, said rather loudly, "Hello, Nigel, trying to decide which side you're on today?"

Nigel ignored Yob and made a beeline for me. He looked me up and down, extended a limp, pudgy hand, and muttered, "Why don't you and I forget politics for a while and go somewhere and get it on?" I didn't fault him for favoring the direct approach, but even putting politics aside, if that were possible, I could hardly have fancied him less.

"Sorry," I told him. "I've got to be home for tea or Aunty will be cross." I'd used this ridiculous excuse before to good effect but it didn't stop Nigel.

"I'm sure there's some convenient corner we could commandeer," he said, looking around furtively. Just as I was beginning to get the creeps, he piped up: "I saw your photos in *Bloke*! The ones of skinheads. Fucking great!" Then suddenly the subject changed yet again: Nigel Peskett seemed to have a very short attention span. "I've got to get to the opera this evening," he informed me. "I want to have a few drinks first. Sure you won't join me, you could probably get a standby."

I declined Nigel's various offers, which seemed to faze him not at all, and he bustled off, his ample buttocks vanishing into the crowd, leaving me not quite knowing what to make of so odd a creature as this queer, opera-

LONDON SKIN & BONES

loving reactionary with green stumps for teeth. Of course I shared none
of this with Susan. But after exchanging a few remarks on the party, the
weather and the state of the country, we elided to the subject of her wayward
younger brother. Susan shrugged and made a weary gesture suggestive of
sad and habitual exasperation.

"When he was young, he was a bit balmy," she reminisced, "but at least
he wasn't a Nazi!"

"He was in GLF, wasn't he," I said.

"Well, not really," Susan answered, drawing her cardigan around her
shoulders. "It was Kenny who was in GLF, Kenny de Jong."

Suddenly my pot-and-gingerbeer-enhanced feelings of benign
relaxation turned to alert attention. I would never have expected to hear
Kenny de Jong's name in connection with either Nigel Peskett *or* the GLF.
Kenny was the youngest and most attractive of the workers at Finsbury
Park's local Lion Garage and machine shop. The Lion was run by a loose-
knit extended family of Rastafarians presided over by the severe and
dessicated figure of George Lewis and his more affable brother Hosiah. As
the Lion Garage was the local supply point for our excellent local grass and
hash, I had occasion to speak with Kenny and his cohorts from time to time.
With big brown eyes, a quiet manner, and dreadlocks usually wrapped in
a brightly colored snood, Kenny was an attractive, boyish-looking fellow,
polite and businesslike, even a little flirtatious but elusive. He kept himself to
himself. His past connection to GLF, and to the chronically disturbed Nigel
Peskett, came as a revelation, and of course I wanted to know more.

Sustained by a large glass of gin and bitters, Susan was in a talkative
mood, and as various party guests wandered through the garden, she told
me the story of Nigel, Kenny, and Mr. Peabody Dredd.

"Nigel in those days started going to meetings of that new gay group,"
Susan reminded me. I had been to a few meetings of the GLF myself before
I went back to Canada. They used to meet in a big old church. The meetings
were held in the main part of the church, but if you were there for the first
time, you were supposed to stay in the hallway outside the main room and
listen to a speech by a severe Marxist professor in a leather jacket and trench
coat. It could get pretty boring, especially as you could hear the laughter
from the livelier meeting in the next room. I remembered seeing Nigel
there, skulking at the back, but we never spoke.

"Nigel started going because Kenny de Jong was going," Susan said,
"and Nigel had a big crush on Kenny."

So Kenny, as I suspected, was not quite as young as he appeared. Or as unworldly.

"In those days," Susan told me, "Kenny was the boyfriend of a minor gangster called George Peabody, who had been a rent-collector for ... what was his name, the slumlord?"

"Peter Rachman?" I ventured.

"Yes, that's the one. Got a light, luv?"

I lit her cigarette and noticed her hand trembled slightly.

"Oh, ta muchly! Peabody did this and that for Rachman and somehow Kenny got mixed up with him. Nigel met Kenny when they were both going to meetings of the GLF."

"Yes," I said. "I went to a few meetings. Never ran into Kenny though. I would have remembered him."

"Good-looking boy," Susan acknowledged.

"I remember Nigel, though."

In GLF days, Susan's brother had been a pale, scrawny youth who dressed in odd, effeminate outfits mixed with quasi-military drag. Not that this weird get-up was all that unusual then but his pasty face and alarming teeth caused him to stand out. He was eventually barred for bringing a loaded gun to a meeting. I suspected Susan might not know this and I saw no reason to alarm her by spilling the beans at this late date.

"Nigel got quite fixated on Kenny," Susan confided. "Kenny was a nice boy but I don't think he was interested. But they did pal up for a while." Susan flicked her cigarette ash into an empty beer can standing in the hollowed-out top of a brightly-colored plaster toadstool. "The problem *was*," she mused, "well, *Peabody* was the problem." Nigel, it seemed, had developed a huge crush on the boyfriend of a well-known minor gangster with a jealous streak. By now I was all ears as Susan continued the story.

"Eventually Nigel got Kenny to take him home, Nigel's flat not being a fit place for man nor beast. Now I don't know what happened, mind you," she was careful to stress. "But I know Nigel had gone to Peabody's flat with Kenny which was bloody stupid of him, but Peabody was supposed to be somewhere else. Nigel couldn't sleep and he was in the bathroom when Peabody unlocked the door and came into the flat."

"That must have made him nervous," I ventured.

"Well, *yes*! He told me he was scared shitless, excuse my French. Kenny was sleeping. All the lights were out but Nigel could see Peabody by the light from the street through the window. Nigel swore he saw Peabody holding something that glinted in the light; he thought it was a razor or a weapon of some kind. Nigel figured Peabody had found out about Nigel's existence and come for him. He didn't wait. He had that stupid gun with him and he fired, and hit Peabody in the face." So she *did* know about the gun! "The bullet went into his cheek, smashed it, went through the bridge of his nose, smashed that, and lodged just north of his right eye." Susan drew her fingers slowly across her face. "Peabody staggered out onto the street where he collapsed."

"Was Nigel charged?" I asked.

"*Nobody* was charged. MAN COLLAPSES IN STREET was the headline in the local paper. *Ridiculous!* Of course he bloody collapsed, he had a bullet in his face! Peabody was taken to hospital and told everyone what a good boy he was, how no one could possibly want to harm him, must have been a terrible accident. I don't suppose he knew Nigel was there, how could he? And he certainly didn't want Kenny involved because Kenny knew all about Peabody's ... well, illegal doings. After that, Nigel gave Kenny a wide berth. Hasn't seen him for years."

"Kenny joined the Rastas," I said. "Wears his hair in dreadlocks done up in one of those handy tea-cozys. Stays pretty close to home now, mends bikes."

"I don't blame him," said Susan blowing another smoke ring in the direction of the hollyhocks. "I'm sure Peabody thinks Kenny shot him. Of course, he calls himself Peabody Dredd now. Peabody Dredd, gangster kingpin! Nigel's afraid of him but I don't think he knows Nigel exists."

I was digesting all this when Aunt Doll tottered over.

"Hello, you two. You all right? Got enough drinks?"

Susan said yes, we were *very* all right and that she was just telling me about Nigel. Aunt Doll threw me a glance and raised her eyebrows and made a little ooh shape with her lips.

"Are you going to be doing the church fair again this year?" Susan asked.

"Yes, I expect so, luv. I always look forward to it." Aunt Doll had a regular card-reading booth at Chipping Ongar's local church bazaar.

"Are you going to be the Sultana Shawarma again this year?"

"Something like that," said Doll. "Maybe Madame Shawarma this time. I've always had a secret desire to be a madam!" She put her hand to her mouth and laughed. Aunt Doll's annual tealeaf-reading and tarot booth was a popular fixture at St. Joseph of Arimathea's (Chipping Ongar). Adorned with a large cairngorme affixed to one of her many turbans, she made, everyone agreed, a fine seer. "Well," she added, "I'm glad of the sit down really. It's a bit of fun and makes a few pounds for the church. Course I don't say everything I see. Supposed to help people, not frighten them! I'll just take these drinks to Mister ..." The forgotten last name was replaced by a gesture with a small tray as she continued down the garden path, swaying a bit because of her bad legs.

Susan stood up and buttoned her cardigan. "I'll say this for Nigel though, he's a bloody good shot! Peabody's lucky he wasn't killed ... *Nigel's* lucky he wasn't killed! Though the way he's going ..." She left the rest unsaid but it was obvious she was worried about her crazy brother who had apparently shot a notorious gangster, gotten away with it, and become a fascist.

At that point Seamus Moore came back and Susan headed into the house to join Poddy, Jean, and a few other people standing around Aunt Doll who was about to launch into her limited but highly varied piano repertoire.

"We were just talking about Susan's brother," I told Seamus, intending to go no further but wondering if he'd have anything to say.

"Nigel Peskett?" Seamus lowered his voice. "He's a right doctor, that one. He'll stitch you up soon as look at you. He's dangerous and all, no telling what he'll do."

"So I hear."

"I wouldn't have anything to do with him if I was you."

We walked over to join Laurie and stood next to him by the garden wall, seeing who could count the most fireflies.

I don't claim to know the truth about Nigel Peskett, Kenny de Jong and Peabody Dredd. I have only Nigel's story, related secondhand by Susan. And of course, it's really none of my business. Nigel continues to give me the beadle eye on the rare occasions when we run into one another. Kenny de Jong continues to sell me grass and flirt mildly with me. Peabody Dredd I saw just the once. Sitting on a barstool talking about football. He looked quite fierce. But of course, looks can be deceiving.

TAKE THESE PEARLS

When I lived in Finsbury Park in the early 80s, I spent many an evening in the back of Boris's stamp shop. The big kitchen behind the high stamp drawers was the favorite hangout of our little group of friends, and the big round wooden table provided a platform for countless discussions, fuelled by corned beef and Branson pickle sandwiches, and mugs of hot tea. Sometimes I found myself there on a Saturday morning as well. My friend Andy and I would get up about ten o'clock and, occasionally accompanied by our landlord Russell, would go around the corner to Ali's café for breakfast. Then Russell would head home to work around the house or see to the chickens, and Andy and I would go to Boris's.

Elliot and Lionel, who were identical brothers, were always there, dark-haired, quiet, conspiratorial, and mischievous. And sometimes Windom Price would drop by carrying his bulging briefcase full of stamp mounts, magnifying glasses, watermark detectors, stockbooks, perforation gauges, and other accoutrements. Windom was a tall man in his forties with a camp manner, a shock of dense, well-brushed hair, a fragrant cloud of cologne, and just a touch of makeup. He had wide, womanly hips. "He has hips like Heydrich," Boris once said, suddenly turning toward me and smiling, his cigarette ash falling into the washing up water.

Windom Price could always be counted on to make a wry comment or a wicked imitation of some pompous politician. His grating, high-pitched Margaret Thatcher impersonation always sent the Triplets into gales of laughter. And his elliptical, wholly invented conversations between Tom Driberg and Lord Boothby always got a chuckle from Boris.

That summer morning he came in the door just as Andy and I were taking off our coats. The Triplets amused themselves making up rhymes: "*Windom Price! / led the mice / on guided tours of Paradise!*"

"You naughty boys!" Windom contributed. "You should both be spanked! Or be made to spank one another!"

"*Windom's going to spank us! Windom's going to spank us!*" crowed Elliot.

"Me first!" shouted Lionel, pouring himself a mug of tea.

"Now pipe down the lot of you," answered Boris, "and see to those West German packets, nice and inexpensive. Make sure there's five from the specials box in every one."

Elliot whispered something to Lionel who replied by elbowing Elliot in the ribs. Soon they were tussling at the table with one another and giggling.

"If you boys are going to fight," piped Windom, "put on jockstraps!"

"I left mine upstairs," replied Elliot. "With my cowboy boots."

"Be a diva instead!" suggested Lionel.

Elliot put down the stamps, scampered over to the junk drawer and pulled out a single, long string of pearls which he twirled about and draped around his neck under his clean white shirt, open to the waist.

"Elliot has the right kind of skin to heal pearls," stated Lionel with a serious look on his face.

"And Lionel ..." Elliot started to say.

"Has the right kind of skin to heal swine!" interjected Windom Price.

We all laughed, including Boris, quickly chiding us too: "What will the customers think?"

"I don't see any at the moment," said Andy. "We can be as disgusting as we like."

"Just wait for a bit," said Windom. "They'll all be pouring through the door when they wake up this morning and there on the breakfast tray lightly flecked with marmalade is your splendid ad on page 23 of the new *Hampstead & Highgate Shoppers News,* for which I again thank you." Windom edited his mother's struggling little paper, to which he contributed a column called "My Favourite Stamps." He took a copy of the new issue from his briefcase and laid it on the counter. He and Boris leaned over it and scrutinized it together.

LONDON SKIN & BONES

"Where are we going tomorrow?" A voice emanated from the sofa where Henk Sonderhausen had been lying, wrapped in a coat and apparently asleep. Sundays were our day to wander—three or four or five of us—through Hampstead Heath, or take the bus to the Bald Faced Stag and cross Epping Forest, or explore some unfamiliar part of the city, always accompanied by sandwiches, thanks to Boris, and plenty of good grass, thanks to our friendly local Rastas.

"Boudicca's Grave!" said Elliot. We always said "Boo-dikka," which we maintained was British, and therefore correct, instead of the high-falutin' Roman "Bo-a-de-see-ya" we were taught in school.

"We went there last week with Yob and Orbit," said Andy. "Took those flowers Mrs. Singh give us."

"She's a bit of an old Boudicca herself, I think, Mrs. Singh," piped Windom, fixing a fresh Sobranie into his tortoiseshell cigarette holder with a theatrical leer.

"A Boudicca manqué?" suggested Boris, glancing over his spectacles.

"What's that mean?" asked Elliot.

Boris pointed to the big dictionary next to the fridge but Elliot was too engrossed in West Germany.

"I have a wonderful new line of stamp hinges," said Windom. "They're *flavoured!* Piña Colada ... Opium ... Tartrate of Vermouth ..."

"Liar!" answered Elliot, laughing. Under his shirt, the strand of pearls glowed incongruously against his skin, reminding me of the day I first saw them lying on Boris's table. And that took me back to my school days at Beal Grammar decades before.

Beal Grammar School was an unexceptional state academy in an old building in Ilford, and for a year or two, one of my friends there was a tall, beefy, scholarly boy with the odd name of Arthur Fothko. In our idle moments, Fothko and I enjoyed making up complicated stories together, but after I started writing them down, he began for some reason to lose interest. It was about that time when Mr. Hyndeman, the games master, suggested I try out for the school running team. Tall and thin, I had the right build for distance running, which as it turned out proved to be my one and only athletic skill. I suggested to Fothko that he try out for the shot put, but was not surprised that the school had never thought to provide one.

I'd noticed in gym class that for such a large boy, he was surprisingly fast off the blocks and for the first few yards of any race was quite impressive;

65

after that his heavy, bulky body quickly weighed him down and ... well, it was all over pretty quickly; he usually came in last. Fothko just wasn't cut out to trot around a track in a pair of baggy shorts. But one day, out of the blue, he challenged me not to a hammer throw or a caber toss, but to a footrace!

That evening we had been hanging about the school. The track was deserted. My grandfather's old stopwatch was hauled from my knapsack to signal the start of the race. As we headed out, Fothko, on the outside lane, began a little ahead. He seemed slow starting and I quickly caught up to him. As I did he left his lane and veered into mine, his heavy bulk pushing me effortlessly off the cinder track and onto the grass verge where I stood gaping at him, wondering what on earth he was up to.

Fothko crossed the finish line alone and, huffing and puffing, loudly announced that he had won! I felt hurt, puzzled, and angry.

"You know that was a foul!" I shouted. "What's the matter with you anyway?" But I had to make up my own answer.

It was the end of our friendship, such as it was. Soon afterwards, my family moved, I left Beal Grammar School and didn't see Arthur Fothko again, or think much about him, until years later, when once again he briefly entered my life.

I was helping out at the Old Sarge's military surplus shop one autumn afternoon when Farouk Wylie came through the door for the first time. Farouk was a slender, strikingly handsome young man who appeared to be in his mid-twenties, with slick, jet black hair, smooth olive skin, highly polished shoes and an expensive looking overcoat. Catching sight of him, I wondered—was he Spanish? Eurasian? Puerto Rican? At any rate, his brilliantine coiffure, studied bearing, and sinuous manner suggested an elegant, old-fashioned gigolo from the pages of Michael Arlen or Dorothy L. Sayers. He certainly seemed out of place in grimy Finsbury Park.

He had come to sell some military badges and medals. Whether he and Sarge came to any agreement I can't remember. But he did strike up a conversation with me about the book I was reading, Laurence Durrell's *Balthazar*, set in the ancient city of Alexandria. It turned out Farouk Wylie had been born there. His mother was an Egyptian woman from a wealthy family; his father, a colonel working for British intelligence, had shot himself when Farouk was very young. We had dinner together that evening at Ali's café, Farouk delighting Ali with a few words of Arabic. I was invited to drop by the family home a few evenings later.

LONDON SKIN & BONES

Farouk Wylie lived in Wanstead, in one of the large, posh, double-fronted houses on Snaresbrook Road across from the Eagle Pond, a spot I knew well from my childhood. His mother, a tall, stately woman, had obviously been a great beauty in her youth (many photos about the house confirmed it) but over the years her youthful hauteur had curdled into cynicism, and her features had become etched with bitterness and disdain. She was polite to me, but without warmth. Did she dislike me as *me*, I wondered, or merely as a representative of some group she disfavored—humanity maybe?

Farouk had told me he and his mother shared their house with his friend Arthur. To my surprise, a few minutes after Mrs. Wylie served tea, biscuits and turkish delight, who should enter the room, fiddling with an unlit pipe, but my old school chum Arthur Fothko, togged out in tweed jacket, carpet slippers, and someone else's old school tie.

What followed was an oddly awkward four-way exchange of small talk, a bit like a bridge game without the cards. When Farouk and his mother left the room to confer with some neighbors, Arthur suddenly adopted a peculiarly confiding attitude, speaking in a near-whisper accompanied by odd little nods and winks. He made no reference to our schooldays at Beal, instead suggesting that he had somehow been "brought in" by the Wylies to organize their various affairs.

"What sort of work do you do then?" I asked.

"Accountancy, estate appraisals, that sort of thing," he replied. "I have a trust fund, of course," he added. (Why "of course"?) "But the damn lawyers won't let me get at it properly ... Ah, here comes Farouk."

His remarks were punctuated by digging at his pipe, tapping the burned tobacco into an ashtray, and cleaning the stem with one of those little plastic swords you get with martinis. The pipe remained unlit throughout. All innocuous enough, of course, but somehow the whole routine seemed false, vain, and pointless, a performance with Fothko himself as his own audience. I felt uncomfortable and made my getaway as soon as I could.

Whatever else Arthur Fothko might have become, there was no doubt he remained an avid reader of obscure and intriguing volumes, and before I left that evening he pressed upon me a book called *Musk, Hashish, and Blood* by Hector France, a collection of Algerian tales with a lurid dust-jacket painting of a busty houri being approached menacingly by a scarlet-clad Arab with a knife.

"No hurry getting it back to me."

Over the next week as I read through *Musk, Hashish, and Blood*, I thought about the Wylies and their domestic arrangements. Farouk had seemed quite fond of Fothko, his gaze occasionally following him around the room, but Fothko's feelings, if any, were even more opaque than Mrs. Wylie's sour disregard. At any rate, the three of them seemed to form a closed system which no one else would ever be able to penetrate or disturb.

A week or so after my visit I went to see Edna and Vera Williams, elderly sisters, old stamp-collecting friends of Boris, who lived above their wool shop in Wanstead High Street and occasionally invited me to dinner. The misses Williams went to bed early, so after a tasty meal of roast beef, Yorkshire pudding and trifle, and an hour or so swapping stamp duplicates, I found myself walking down High Street toward Snaresbrook tube station. I had finished the last chapter of *Musk, Hashish, and Blood* on my way over. Pasted into the book (oddly, inside the back cover) was a bookplate showing a wreath of acanthus leaves and rifles around the inscription "Ex Libris Col. C.W. Wylie." I decided to make a short detour and drop the volume off at the Wylies before heading home.

It was cool and foggy that evening. The Eagle Pond was quiet and deserted, the swans on their island for the night, the ducks apparently asleep, and only a single pair of moorhens paddling about through the mist that floated across the pond. As I crossed the street and headed toward the house, a taxi pulled up in front of the gate, disgorging Mrs. Wylie and Arthur Fothko, giggling and clinging to each other, with Mrs. Wylie perhaps a bit unsteady on her feet. I stopped a few yards from the house, hidden, I was sure, by the darkness and the fog, and watched them totter, laughing, toward the front door.

I'll let them get their coats off before I ring the bell, I thought, and sat down beside one of the big old trees beside the Eagle Pond. I lit a half-smoked joint from my pocket, and sat for a few minutes, enjoying the cool night and the familiarity of the spot I'd known since I'd lived with my family in the council estate nearby. I finished my smoke and headed across the street again.

The house was quite dark, apart from the outside lantern and one upstairs window light. Suddenly I heard loud voices coming from an upper room—a male voice and a shrill cry from Mrs. Wylie: "Get out! Get out!" I retreated into the high hedges in time to see Arthur Fothko come out the front door carrying a briefcase, walk down the path, and disappear down Snaresbrook Road.

Obviously, this was no time to show up with a smile and a borrowed book. I scribbled a note saying, "Thanks! Sorry you weren't in," and left the book propped up inside the front storm door.

Two weeks later, I was back at Boris's sorting stamps when Farouk Wylie walked through the door, elegant and handsome as ever in a sharp suit, highly polished shoes, and a stylish shoulder bag. I invited him into the big back kitchen behind the stamp drawers and made him a cup of tea. As we sat at the big table, he told me Fothko had left the Wylie house, taking with him a pearl necklace that his mother had once showed them both, telling them it had been a valuable gift from an old admirer.

Boris joined us as Farouk fished around in his shoulder bag and brought out a single strand of pearls. They lay, white and gleaming against a cleared spot on the walnut table.

"It's funny," he said. "The necklace had four strands of pearls. I remembered Mumma had broken one of them and the pearls from the broken strand were all in a little box in a drawer. After Fothko disappeared with the rest of the necklace, I thought I would have what was left restrung for Mumma. I found the pearls in her drawer—and I found this too."

He held a yellowing newspaper clipping between two fingers. Boris took it carefully and put on his reading glasses. The clipping, from an East End newspaper, was dated 1962. It was a brief item about the opening of a new, upmarket nightclub in the Mile End Road; it was called Kentucky and owned by the Kray twins, well-known gangsters of the time. A photo showed a laughing Reggie Kray with his arm around a beautiful young woman with a drink in her hand. Another man stood beside her, apparently talking to her. The woman was Mrs. Wylie—and she was wearing the necklace, with its four strands of pearls.

"Reggie Kray!" exclaimed Boris. "Was he your mother's admirer, then?"

"I don't know," said Farouk.

Boris rubbed his chin and took off his glasses. "Tell me," he said, "Do you know if the theft was ... reported? To the police?"

"No," Farouk answered. "Mumma just dismissed the whole thing with a wave of her hand and that little 'pfftt' sound she makes as much to say, 'It's of no importance.' I found out why when I went to get them restrung. They're not real! Just very good fakes."

When Farouk left I walked him to the door and, to my surprise, he kissed me on the lips as he stood on the step.

"Let's get together soon," he said, running his finger down my shirt front. "You know where to find me."

As he headed down the street, my friend Andy arrived in full skinhead attire—jeans, newly pressed shirt, suspenders, and highly polished Doc Martens. My thoughts rapidly detached themselves from the nattily dressed Farouk and followed Andy, smelling slightly of Lifebuoy soap, into the shop.

"Boris! You have pearls!" Andy noticed the single strand of pearls lay on the table among the tea mugs, stamp packets, and disassembled copies of *Gay Sunshine* and *The Hampstead and Highgate Shoppers News.* "Have you been swapping stamps for jewellery again?"

"I'll give them back to Farouk when I see him," I said.

"I don't think he wants them," smiled Boris.

Andy picked up the pearls and draped them around Boris's neck.

"I'm ready for my night out!" said Boris, batting his eyelashes, and proceeding to do the washing up.

"I'm dying for a cup of tea," said Andy.

"There's one in the pot," indicated Boris. "It seems your old friend Fothko ended up with a load of junk jewellery!" He threw the wet dish towel onto a tray and unfolded a fresh one. "Do you think Farouk's mother might be a somewhat *calculating* lady?"

Andy and I were still in the shop later that night, sorting through a missionary lot in a huge sack, when the Old Sarge came by. As Sarge joined us at the table, Boris was standing with his back to the window, smoking, holding his cigarette like a pipe in the Russian manner. That night his habitual outfit of gray flannels, work shirt and ratty cardigan was augmented, most unusually, by a single strand of pearls. Sarge, being Sarge, never mentioned it.

In the weeks following, I phoned the Snaresbrook house several times but got no answer. Then one Saturday afternoon, Farouk Wylie showed up at the door of the house I lived in on Turle Road. The brilliantine had gone from his hair, and he was dressed in corduroys and loafers. I invited him up to my room. When we got there, Andy was lying on my bed reading a battered paperback of *A Kid for Two Farthings.* He gave Farouk a quick appraisal and broke open three bottles of warm beer from the cupboard.

A couple of hours later, most of our clothes lay around the room or draped over the big armchair. Both Farouk and I were exhausted, while

LONDON SKIN & BONES

Andy, posing in only socks and boots in front of the mirror, boasted he was "just getting started." When he caught sight of the mantlepiece clock, he suddenly remembered: "Geez, I'm spozed to be laying carpets in Romford in forty-five minutes!" He was dressed and out the door in a small whirlwind.

After Andy had fled, Farouk lay on my bed drinking the last of the beer, and grew confidential.

"I don't think Fothko actually *stole* the pearls. Well, maybe he did. At first Mumma said, 'He's gone ... and taken my pearls with him.' Then later she said she told him to 'take the pearls and go!' She said, 'Oh, Farouk, I want you to have a companion. I lost *my* companion. But Farouk, believe me, this one was not for you. There was ... something missing from him. He is dangerous ... without being interesting.'"

Farouk asked his mother if the pearls had really been a gift from Reggie Kray. "No," she said. "I barely knew Reggie Kray. They were from his brother Ronnie. Ronnie was queer, you know, and it was Ronnie I was friendly with for a while when I was young and foolish and before they both got sent up for murder. One night we were out with one of Ronnie's boyfriends, we'd all three had a few drinks and were horsing around through the streets. I saw the pearls in the window of a junk shop and Ronnie bought them for me, just for a lark. They only cost a few pounds. Your father was away, poor man. I was bored and we were just having fun ... Of course, Arthur thought they were real."

"You *told* him they were real."

"Well ... I let him think ..."

Farouk took a last swig of beer. "I didn't tell you yet."

"What?"

"I got a job. In a bank! I started last week. One of my father's old friends helped Mumma to get it for me. I couldn't really say no."

"What's it like?"

"Oh, it's a terrible bore."

"Think you'll stick at it?"

"For a while maybe. If I can have a bit of fun with it ... shake things up a bit."

"How *is* your mother anyway?" I asked.

"Better than I've seen her in a long while. She has a new boyfriend. Armenian chap, quite nice. He seems to be really bringing her out of herself. Oh, I'm getting my own maisonette down the West End. Small but quite posh. You'll have to come visit once I'm set up. I'll cook one of my fancy curries."

"OK."

He grinned at me over his empty beer glass. Stretched out on the white sheet, his sleek, naked body with its smooth chest and thighs and jet black pubic hair somehow suggested olives and seaweed and warm southern places. I imagined him as a swimsuit model, or running a chic restaurant on the Riviera. Would he really spend his life in a London bank?

As if reading my thoughts, he said quietly, "Nicky ... that's Mumma's new beau ... says if I do OK at the bank for a year or so, I can come work for him in his importing company." He crossed his long legs.

"What does he import?"

"Carpets and pistachio nuts and things ..." He crossed his ankles and raised his eyebrows. "In the meantime ... our office party is next week. Come with me!"

"What, to the party?"

"Yes! *Come as my boyfriend!* I want to have some fun with this dull job or I'll quit in a week and then what would Mumma say? She'd be fit to spit! And I'd *never* get to work for Nicky. So will you be my date?"

"You could always ask Andy."

"Andy, I think, would be a bit much for them at the bank."

"You think so?

"Maybe I should take you both!" He laughed and jumped up, throwing an arm around my shoulder. "Oh, don't be so serious. Be my date, we'll have a great time! Give all those stuffy bankers and snippy office girls something to talk about!"

"Well, Farouk, I must tell you, I'm a bit short of suits and ties."

"It's only a *party*, it's not *formal!* You're not going to be *knighted* for God's sake!"

"Well ..."

"Oh, come on!"

I should go, I thought: a simple enough request, to attend a party with a friend. On the other hand, I wasn't *really* his boyfriend. Was I? Or were Farouk's silky charms—those long eyelashes, those smooth thighs!—ever so gently leading me into a game, a harmless little game, of slightly false pretenses?

As it happened, I didn't hear from Farouk Wylie for a while. But about

LONDON SKIN & BONES

six weeks later I spotted Windom Price whispering his customary prayer over a plate of scrambled eggs at Ali's café.

"Guess who I ran into!" he challenged, pointing his fork in my direction.

"Elephant Boy!"

"All right, I'll tell you. Farouk Wylie! I had to go to that stamp shop near St. Pancras station and ducked into that nice tea place around the corner for a few minutes to refresh myself. Anyway, there was Farouk looking terribly louche in an expensive suit. On his way to *Paris,* he said. With just a briefcase! Seems he left his job and ran off with some millionaire."

"*Millionaire!*" I echoed.

"Yes, some foreign chap. Used to be married to Farouk's mother apparently ... Is that considered incest?"

"No, I don't think so, Windom. Well, maybe symbolic incest."

Ali, who had been half-listening to our conversation, interjected, "Are you fellows talking naughty again?"

"No, Ali," said Windom, "we are *not* talking naughty. We are gossiping."

Ali leaned over and refilled our cups of tea from a big white enamel pot. "Then you will need more tea. You fellows are such good customers!"

MRS. SINGH'S TANDOORI POPCORN

Funny how some small thing, a little sign, a token, a half-forgotten item of no particular importance from the past, can unexpectedly be brought back to memory. Suddenly what had been almost inconsequential now seems fraught with significance. It was that way with the flag. It had been just a funny novelty, leaning in a corner with the other flags and painted signs, part of the clutter in the front store-room of Boris Mostaynko's stamp shop, a dim room full of discarded furniture, unread books, boxes of mismatched crockery, and machines awaiting repair. It was only after its loss and retrieval that we started calling it "the Skin & Bones" and prizing it like some regimental standard.

The flag had started its life as an ordinary, commercially printed banner, bought in a street market and supposedly imitative of the pirate flags of old—black with a white skull over a pair of crossed bones. But one of Boris's young friends, a squatter in one the abandoned buildings beyond the tube station, had a girlfriend who liked to sew appliquéd quilts and bits of collaged artwork; she had changed the regulation skull to the face of a grinning, handsome skinhead, with a missing tooth and a little crossed bandaid on his near-bald head, echoing the crossed bones beneath. Pinned to the wall or fluttering in the wind, it looked suitably cheeky and defiant. But the young squatter had moved away, the girlfriend too, with or without him, and the Skin & Bones had been relegated to the haphazard flag collection. Leaning in a corner, fastened to a plastic mop-handle, it was generally ignored.

"Our banner looked suitably cheeky and defiant."

Then the rally came. It was late in what had been a wet English summer, but in the past few days, the weather had changed, and we all wanted to take advantage of the sun and warmth. In those early years of Mrs. Thatcher's regime, our scruffy scrap of London provided little in the way of excitement, or even entertainment. For that, there were excursions to various street markets and bookshops, near and far, long walks in Epping Forest or shorter ones on Hampstead Heath, and the occasional poetry reading or cobbled-together dramatic performance. My Uncle Fred and Aunt Esther would sometimes invite me to dinner. And once in a while, a few of us would walk or take a bus to the Roundhouse to drink mugs of tea with the leatherboys who rode in on their bikes. Most of the time we worked at our day jobs, sat in the kitchen in the back of Boris's stamp shop, spent most of our pay on groceries, and stayed close to home to make our wages stretch through the week. What little money we had left over we pooled to buy grass at preferred rates from the Rastas at the Lion Garage. We enjoyed one another's company and kept pretty much to ourselves.

So when Seamus Moore strode into the shop, announcing in his booming voice that he would be reading one of his funny, scurrilous political poems at a rally at Mile End in the heart of the old working class East End of London, even the least political of us was glad to go; it would provide a bit of entertainment at the cost of a few bus tickets. As well as being a public poet, Seamus Moore was a fellow member of the tiny Finsbury Park Anarchist group, another of whose adherents was one of the organizers. The precise grievance, or series of grievances, that prompted the rally I am ashamed to say I have forgotten, as Mrs. Thatcher and her Conservatives were unpopular with us for so many reasons. It may have been to do with housing conditions and the fact that so many of us had no proper place to live. (Most of us favored London's left-wing mayor "Red" Ken Livingstone, later unceremoniously removed from office by the Iron Lady.) We had all heard "The Ballad of London Bridge" (or bits of it) before of course during rinse cycles at Mrs. Singh's laundrette, over breakfast at Ali's café or over drinks at the Four Kings. But this was the first time it would be presented as intended—declaimed to an assembled crowd in a public square—albeit a square considerably smaller and more obscure than Trafalgar. I didn't want to miss it.

I was born in London (during a particularly ferocious V-weapons air raid toward the end of The War) and as the 1980s approached had settled in the working-class district of Finsbury Park in North-East London after spending years in Canada with my parents. After coming back to my birthplace on a visit, I had been keen to rediscover London and its old familiar places. I became involved in the gay movement and met a good-looking and congenial boyfriend. My academic career, which had begun so promisingly, had fizzled out for a number of reasons, one of them being that the main aim of it—to gain some teaching credentials—turned out to be rather misguided. In those days, no one who was openly gay was permitted to teach at any level, from kindergarten to graduate school. And I knew myself well enough to realize that I would be miserable trying to lead a closeted life. I dropped out.

A subsequent career as a microfilm photographer at the University of Toronto allowed me to save some money, and what began as a vacation trip extended itself into a new life in my old boyhood haunts. My puzzled parents were somewhat mollified by the proximity of my aunt and uncle and a few other relatives, while my diminishing savings, plus a few extra Pounds earned from photographs and book reviews, cushioned the blow of a much lowered standard of living. My affair with the boyfriend soon petered out, due in part to his proselytizing Marxism, which bored me, and his heavy smoking, which made kissing unpleasant. Finsbury Park beckoned, as it was the cheapest part of London that was not considered dangerous. Bleak and dirty on the surface, it nevertheless housed some very congenial people, one of whom was the aforesaid Seamus Moore, a volatile and somewhat unpredictable man in his fifties, manager of the Finsbury Park Men's & Boys' Boxing Club, whom some regarded as a nuisance or a scourge, but whom I found to a kind, loyal, and generous friend.

The good weather held on the day of the rally, and four or five of us took the tube into the East End, carrying with us a plain black banner, a Union Jack, and the made-over pirate flag on its ugly white plastic pole. As it turned out, I knew the little square quite well as it fronted on the old Russian Baths where Boris Mostayenko and his Eastern European cronies sometimes took the waters. Directly across the square was a boarded-up brick building whose steps provided a handy dais for speakers and performers to hold forth.

While the rest of our party made their way to the front of the gathering, I looked around to see if I could spot anyone I knew. I caught sight of a small knot of familiar faces: Squiffy Haltergeist ran the local flat rental agency, catering mostly to foreign students and guestworkers. He was a

IAN YOUNG

pudgy, ginger-haired man, going bald, with thick spectacles and teeth that stuck out at odd angles, making spittle-spray an unavoidable hazard. Squiffy was sharing a cigarette with two self-employed Finsbury Park locals whose carefully inked index cards usually decorated the notice board in the local tobacconists. The Vile Bitch (a professional name), whose advertisements announced her trade as a dominatrix, was a large, loud, friendly, fortyish woman with dyed black hair and a good figure, wrapped in a sturdy green mackintosh. Off duty, she looked no different from any High Street housewife. Hovering beside her was her friend Florence, a skinny, dark-skinned individual of uncertain gender wearing Bowie boots and an Afro wig. Florence (professional name Lady Buckmaster) was swigging a bottle of ginger beer.

"Hello, Squiffy. Hello, Vi, Florence."

I declined the offers of tobacco and ginger beer.

"Ss-supposed to rain later," said Squiffy, grinning and drooling slightly. "They say Tom Robinson's going to play!"

Robinson was a popular out-of-the-closet gay performer, best known for the upbeat anthem "Glad to be Gay." I had met him at the launch of Gay Men's Press a year or so earlier and had been impressed that, unlike so many rock stars, he seemed still to be a real person, living in the real world, not just the artificial ego-inflating universe of show business.

"His band broke up," Vile informed me.

"I'm sorry to hear that," I said.

"The Shadows! That's the band for me!" Vile pronounced, naming the anodyne backup band on early Cliff Richard productions.

"They say Cliff is going into politics," I murmured, which drew raucous laughs from Vile and Squiffy and no reaction at all from Florence.

"Be careful," Squiffy warned. "Nigel and his lot are wandering about. I wouldn't get in their way if I were you."

I thanked him for the information. Nigel Peskett was a blotchy-faced local character in the Park, ringleader of a small gang of crypto-fascist hooligans. Squiffy, someone had told me, had been at grammar school with him. The rally was late to start and featured a series of uninspiring speakers who thankfully were kept to a few minutes each. Before the small crowd could become too restive, Tom Robinson emerged from nowhere onto the steps, said a few words, and launched into "Up Against the Wall," which got everyone singing along.

LONDON SKIN & BONES

I wandered about, checking out the crowd, and saw our little group, banners held high, toward the front. After a few minutes of Tom Robinson, who promised to return before the end of the demo, another speaker introduced Seamus Moore as "the internationally known poet" which was news to me. Seamus, wearing his trademark army greatcoat and a fedora, boomed out "The Balled of London Bridge" in its entirety, which pleased the crowd no end.

"The word came down
from Maggie the bitch:
she said steal from the poor
and give to the rich!
And all the filthy blighters
and the dirty little shiters
all came crawling out from under
the piles of London Bridge ..."

I stayed for the rest of Seamus's poem but as I have a low tolerance for crowds and speeches, left to reconnoiter the area before Tom Robinson's second set. As a result I missed the scuffle beside the Russian Baths that resulted in the loss of the homemade Skin & Bones.

A week later I was sitting in the front passenger seat of Rose Madison's little sardine can of a car on the way to Barkingside, between us a big bag of homemade tandoori popcorn from Mrs. Singh. Rose was the painter sometimes known as Rose Madder. She was a small woman with the lined face of a heavy smoker and favored trim slacks and colorful berets. We had worked together when I first came back to the city. I had lived on the fringe of Barkingside with my parents years before on one of our several aborted attempts to return to England from various outposts of Empire. Every weekday I made the trip from Beal Grammar school in Ilford, walking the last leg of the journey from the Hainault tube station along the New North Road to Fencepiece Road and our house on Aragon Drive. In those days most of the surrounding properties were still farm fields. Now they had been largely filled in but one sizeable plot remained, an area of vegetable allotments surrounded by a brick wall. This was the preserve of Ted Granger, the groundskeeper, who lived and worked in the only building on the site, a modest one-story brick structure, once a storehouse but long made over into a plain but cozy dwelling.

Ted was a burly, amiable old man, a former merchant seaman and hospital orderly, who presided over the locals' small plots with the assistance of a black and white bull terrier called Bob. Our mission, Rose's and mine, was to pick up several large bags of otherwise redundant carrots, parsnips, and assorted vegetables which Rose, Boris, and I would divvy up. Ted waved and Bob gave a perfunctory bark as we drove up to the gate. It was the only time I had shown up to find Ted not leaning on a spade. He seemed at his happiest when digging in the soil, though his large, tobacco-stained fingers were bent stiff with arthritis.

On the journey from Finsbury Park to Barkingside, Rose (who always seemed to know the latest gossip) had been filling in some details about the excitement I had missed by leaving the rally early. Rose's information overlapped with my own but still left the essential piece of the puzzle unsolved. Apparently Nigel Peskett and a couple of his crypto-fascist pals had caused some sort of disturbance on the fringe of the rally and had engaged some of our lads in a pushing and shoving contest. Nothing terribly violent, said Rose, but enough to annoy everyone and precipitate a chase around the back of the Russian Baths and down the street. When our lads got back to the site of the rally and prepared to head home, it was discovered that one of our flags—the piratical Skin & Bones—was missing. The loss resulted in much swearing and speculation, the consensus being that one of Peskett's boys had stayed behind and swiped the flag while the rest of our lot were engaged in the chase through the neighborhood. In the week that followed I heard much moaning around the big table in Boris's kitchen. Suddenly the patchwork flag which no one had ever taken much notice of had become a valuable icon, an important standard which honor demanded be found and retrieved. My suggestion that we simply make a new one was dismissed as unacceptable by everyone except Boris, who just shrugged, smiled, and continued with the washing up.

As we pulled into the allotment drive I saw that Ted had lit the firepit in front of his home and had arranged several captain's chairs for our comfort.

"There's baked potatoes and chestnuts here." he informed us, "so make yourselves at home." Ted's resources were modest but he was a good host. I knew that as with earlier visits, there would also be tea, home brew, and warm ginger beer. As we sat ourselves down by the fire, another friend emerged from Ted's shelter. Piers Dragonheart (the Piers was legitimate, the Dragonheart his own invention) was a good looking young fellow in his early twenties with dark curly hair and a permanently lopsided stance. His girlfriend of several months was apparently quite well off, from the Woodford horsey set, and his father, Mr. Lee, was owner or part-owner of the Wanstead Riding School opposite Snaresbrook tube station. But it amused Piers to occasionally drive about on top of a horse-drawn wagon in a brightly colored scarf, selling various cut-rate goods and collecting materials for recycling. This of course made him a great favorite of the local children. No wagon was in evidence that day and it became apparent that Piers had been staying with Ted, helping him out with various chores. We all settled down to our small feast, trying not to burn our fingers on the roasted chestnuts. It was a cool night but pleasant nonetheless, and Ted's home brew made the company mellow.

Whenever I dropped by Ted Granger's allotments, Bob the dog insisted on walking me around the perimeter of the property, proudly showing off his preserve, it seemed, to a familiar guest. I left the others to their conversation and dutifully followed the terrier through the patches of root vegetables, along the hollyhock borders and past the compost pile, Bob stopping occasionally to lift a leg or snuffle at a new scent.

When I got back to Ted, Rose, and Piers, they were discussing Squiffy Haltergeist's missing fifty Pounds. Squiffy, it seems, to augment his income from flat referrals, had rented out the two upstairs rooms of his house. One tenant, Benjy, had been ensconced for some time and had given no problems. But a couple of weeks earlier a second young fellow, Joe, had moved in and immediately afterwards Squiffy had been disturbed to find that fifty Pounds in notes (a week's wages for some of us) had vanished from the pocket of a jacket he'd left over a kitchen chair. He had apparently confided in Rose about the matter and asked for her advice.

"He says he can't believe Benjy took it so it could only have been Joe," Rose suggested. But, she said, Joe came highly recommended by no less a judge of character than my employer, the Old Sarge. Sarge's military surplus store drew various young men as the supply of German T-shirts, Yugoslavian combat pants and British Army pullovers could be had quite cheaply. Sarge, unlike Boris, was not one to encourage lingering or extended discussion. But he could be relied on for tips on accommodation and other useful connections. When young Joe, something of a regular customer, had come in looking for a place to stay, Sarge had put him in touch with Squiffy.

When the fifty Pounds had gone missing, Squiffy phoned Sarge in a tizzy.

"If Sarge figured this fellow was honest," I offered, "I'd be inclined to believe it. Sarge is a pretty good judge of character."

Piers had been listening to all this gossip in silence, his large eyes taking it all in.

"Joe they call Cowboy Joe, right?" he said. Piers lived in Wanstead but knew our Finsbury Park crowd pretty well.

"Is he honest, do you think?" I asked.

He didn't answer but asked a question of his own.

"Do you remember when he got beaten up on the street? Lucky someone came along or he would have been badly hurt." I had no knowledge of the incident but Rose remembered it.

"Yes," she said. "Terrible, terrible. He was with that black chap, the one who was barred from the Lion Garage."

Piers nodded. "Yes, you put your finger on it," he said, sticking his face into the steam arising from his baked potato and grinning broadly. "Our friend Cowboy Joe was in a bad district with dubious company." He blew on a piece of potato and gave it to Bob who was waiting patiently by his feet. "He may be honest but ... he's been crashing here and there for a bit, hasn't he. So what does he do when he finally gets his own place? Light up the incense? Put the kettle on? Adopt a kitten? No, I don't think so." Piers's expressive eyes lit up and he flashed a grin. "He goes out into the street and comes back with some dubious piece of trade!"

"So Joe's not a thief," I suggested. "He's just a bit too innocent for his own good."

"Wouldn't be surprised. Anyway, Squiffy's a bit of an innocent himself and if he's going to rent out rooms, he shouldn't leave money lying around."

"I don't know," said Rose. "Stolen property, missing money, it's all too sad. I had a boyfriend once who had light fingers. He was a lovely chap otherwise."

"I remember him," Ted mumbled, pouring tea. "Took you quite a while to get over him."

"I didn't want to get over him," replied Rose, "I wanted to get under him!" Her face crinkled up as she laughed her loud, cackling laugh, and we laughed with her.

We sat about, the four of us, gossiping and enjoying the chestnuts and popcorn as the evening began to grow darker. At one point a man pulled up on a bicycle. It was Tommy Noakes, curly-haired, nimble, and slightly sweaty. In his bike basket he carried several neatly folded pairs of woolen socks in a brown paper bag and some meaty bones wrapped in newspaper.

Tommy and his mate Seamus lived in the two upper floors of an old house opposite the local C. of E. church. The ground floor was the precinct of the landlady, Mrs. Cricheloe, a woman of a certain age, which is to say an uncertain age, who dressed for the most part in black and purple and resembled one of those grand Iberian ladies in mantillas who pop up every now and then on Spanish stamps. Formidable in aspect, Mrs. Cricheloe was actually a kind and friendly person who took a particular interest in the care and feeding of the many stray cats who made homes for themselves in straw-lined boxes in a little-visited section of the churchyard. As she was not always up to walking abroad, this task, among others, was usually delegated to Seamus and Tommy. If you visited their house, you would often find the front door open so as you walked up the path you could see Mrs. Cricheloe ensconced in a large, comfortable chair at the bottom of the stairs in the front hall, flanked by two robust animals she called her "Fou dogs." These were a pair of large chow-chows—one male and black (Pongo), one female and reddish-brown (Moomin). Should the oncoming visitor be unfamiliar, these two would each emit a low, throaty growl, at first resembling a cat's purr but quickly building rather dramatically to a deep, alarming rumble that would deter anyone foolish enough to be harboring evil intentions. A word or two from Mrs. Cricheloe was enough to silence the chows into watchful wariness. Friendlier faces were greeted by curious snuffles (from the dogs, not their owner), and Mrs. Cricheloe would briefly hold court before ushering you upstairs with a wave of a bejewelled hand. Her charitable endeavors were not reserved for cats and dogs alone; she was an accomplished and assiduous knitter, specializing in woolen socks, which her tenants were beseeched to distribute to the needy majority of North-East London.

Tommy delivered breathless greetings all round, proudly handed Ted the bag of socks along with the bones for Bob, and apologized profusely for not being able to stay.

"I was at Boris's today," he said, declining Ted's offer of food and drink. "They got that pirate flag back!" This surprised me as I was sure it had gone for good. I asked what had happened but Ted didn't know, saying I'd have to ask Boris. He peddled away with a bag of tomatoes in his bike basket.

As it grew darker and cooler, Rose and I prepared to leave. Piers was obviously staying on. As we left, Ted presented each of us with a pair of socks, keeping a particularly gaudy red and green pair for himself. "I'll be Father Christmas again!" he promised.

Gathering up our socks and vegetables, we climbed into Rose's car and headed home.

In the warmth of the car, Rose, who didn't like to drive in the dark, was uncharacteristically quiet, and I began to nod off, thinking of old Ted and Bob, happy in their brick hut in their little world. As if reading my thoughts, Rose told me that the allotments Ted managed were yet another of the various properties owned by Marcus Grumbacher, the distinguished numismatic expert who was the sleeping partner in Boris's stamp shop. Marcus, as well as being a numismatist, had made his original fortune in his native Liechtenstein by, as he put it, "taking advantage of certain anomalies in the international platinum market." He had gone on to invest in rundown properties in selected districts all over London. Bringing them up to standard, he then rented them out at generous rates—and eventually sold them to great advantage when their neighborhoods came up in the world. Ted was yet another beneficiary of Marcus's entrepreneurial shrewdness.

I was mulling this over when Rose let me off at the house on Turle Road. She would drop Boris's supplies off, she said, before going home. I headed into our ground floor kitchen with two bags of root vegetables and what was left of the popcorn. The house was quiet and in the kitchen one of the other tenants was making toast. Phil and his boyfriend Desmond shared a room on the middle floor. They took casual work as cooks and servers in various institutions, including our local education factory, the grim-looking George Orwell Secondary School. While I put the vegetables away, Phil regaled me with depressing school stories as the stack of toast grew higher.

"Andy's upstairs," he informed me. Phil had at first been nervous of Andy, the handsome skinhead who had the room next to mine. But once he realized that contrary to stereotype, Andy was neither a Nazi nor a hooligan, but merely a working lad with a rent-boy past, he had mellowed toward him. "You'll find him very pleased with himself."

"Why's that?" I asked him.

"He got Boris's flag back—the one that got stolen at the demo. I said he must've taken on Peskett's entire gang in a fight to the finish but he said, "No, he just used his boyish charms!" Phil raised his eyebrows and headed upstairs, his plate of toast for two balanced precipitously.

LONDON SKIN & BONES

I mopped up Phil's crumbs and headed up to the top floor. As I turned my key in the lock, I could tell by the light under the door that Andy was already in my room. He was sitting on the sofa with his feet in a basin of hot water, fiddling with a Rubik's Cube.

"Have you seen this? It's the latest thing. It's quite fiendish. I've been trying to work it out for an hour and I'm nowhere near figuring it out."

"I brought you socks," I announced. "From Tommy and Mrs. Cricheloe. *And,*" I added, "Mrs. Singh's tandoori popcorn!" Andy was still playing with his cube. "Phil said you retrieved the Skin & Bones."

"I did. I did."

"Is there a story?" I inquired.

"No," he answered, "but I let Phil think there was. I just got it from Squiffy. It wasn't stolen at all. In the chase around the buildings with Nigel's lads, someone must have dropped it. Some friend of Squiffy's found it and gave it to Squiffy. Me and Squiffy, we go back a ways and he phoned me up to come get it. I took it to Boris's and he kissed me on both cheeks like a French general."

"Well," I said, "that's all right, then. All's well that ends well. Have some of Mrs. Singh's tandoori popcorn." Preoccupied with the perplexing colored cube, Andy seemed disinterested but soon dipped into the popcorn bag. Once he got a taste, I knew he wouldn't stop until it was empty.

THE BOY
IN THE BLUE BOXING GLOVES

He danced around the empty ring, making quick little jabs with his left. I hadn't seen him at the Club before, though I had caught a glimpse of him, once, in the neighborhood. He was warming up, I guess, and maybe just getting comfortable in the ring. The first few times you're in the ring you pretty much have to measure the ring with your steps, so you know where you are and where your corner is and how far you are from the ropes. When I say "you," I mean *you* and not me because I've never been in the ring in my life and don't intend to be in the future. I have the wrong build for it and more to the point I've had my share of facial surgery already and have been a card-carrying coward for so long it would be a shame to turn in my membership now.

He was certainly pretty. A lithe little flyweight with a snub nose and a lock of blond hair falling deliciously over his brow. He wore a light blue undervest and a none-too-loose pair of very fetching navy blue shorts. And blue boxing gloves, so blue they were almost fluorescent. They must have been his own as the Finsbury Park Men's and Boys' Boxing Club had certainly never seen such a swank pair. I watched him for a minute as he darted about like a dragonfly wondering where to light. He paid me no mind.

I didn't know his name. I had seen him once outside the Lion Garage talking to Kenny de Jong while tinkering with a bicycle. It was about three weeks later and there he was again, this time at the Men's & Boys', not far from Turle Road and the rooming house where I lived. After letting myself in, I headed to the manager's office to pick up the small parcel earmarked for delivery that A.M. to another club—this one in Mile End near the old Russian Baths.

That early in the morning it was chilly in the Club. The old wooden fans turned slowly under the high tin ceiling and through the gloom a few pale fluorescent lights flickered. The back of the club accommodated Seamus Moore's office in an upper story accessed by a bannistered corridor running across the width of the building. From the open corridor you had a good view of the ring and much of the main floor. I entered the office through the fire escape and the back door, picked up the package with my name on it from Seamus's desk, and stepped out the front way onto the narrow parapet. The main room below was not completely deserted.

Tommy Noakes, a curly-haired journeyman middleweight in his thirties, was sitting on a stool, dressed in a gray sweatshirt, boxing boots, and shorts. Crouching on a lower stool in front of him was a big, bearded man in a pullover, gray flannels, and plastic sandals. This was Seamus Moore, the Club's sole paid employee. Tommy's eyes were closed and he was nodding his head gently, slowly, as Seamus droned away to him while rhythmically slapping and rubbing Tommy's thighs and lower legs with liniment from a bottle. From my perch in the crowsnest above I couldn't hear what Seamus was saying as he kneaded and patted and growled. For a few moments I watched the two old friends, relaxed in what was probably a regular routine, one I'd never observed before. Together in their own world, they seemed not to see or hear me up above them, and rather than disturb their intimate communion, I ducked back into the office and left the way I came in, down the back fire escape and into the laneway.

I needed a cup of coffee to wake me up and headed to Ali's, the local caff. Early morning was the only time Ali's was sure to be crowded, full of assorted men, and one or two women, who'd stopped for breakfast or a hot drink on their way to work. As I waited in line, I changed my mind and decided to order a cocoa for an extra penny. Though the arborite tables were crowded, the customers sat wherever they wished, plonking themselves down unceremoniously next to strangers in the English manner, unlike North Americans who considered it a breach of etiquette, almost an impertinence, to sit at another person's table, even one with several empty chairs. I was about to join a pair of silent workmen when I heard a familiar voice summoning me to share a corner table.

"You're up early!" I said, surprised to see Yob and Orbit who were tucking into plates of curried baked beans on toast, a specialty of the house. Orbit's original name was Rodney. He came from a Romford Jewish family called Bleiberg, distant relatives of the first heart-transplant patient (the operation was a success but the patient died). A hefty, slow, ungainly boy with a Levantine countenance, a lazy eye, and bad acne, he was not usually quick enough to understand anyone's jokes but if others were laughing he was always happy to laugh with them. Orbit was a regular at Boris Mostoyenko's stamp shop where he assiduously soaked stamps off envelope corners and devoured the cheese with beetroot and corned beef with Branson pickle sandwiches. He had a reputation of being very easily distracted, and it was a rule that he was *not* to be left alone in the kitchen as he was inclined to turn the stove on and then forget about it.

Orbit lived in a squat—an abandoned house with a concealed entrance through a back window. His companion Yob was what skinheads called a chickenhead, with a mohawk haircut dyed blue and ripped clothing that was—or appeared to be—held together by safety pins. Orbit was utterly beguiled by Yob's varied tattoos which covered much of his chest and back and encroached onto his neck. As Yob was tall, skinny, and rather frail looking, he benefited from Orbit's heft and surprising physical strength. It was Orbit's strength that gave Fred Dyer, proprietor of the local pub, the Four Kings, his idea for another of his mixed bag of "special events."

I drank my cocoa as I sat talking with Yob and Orbit. Yob was wearing his turtleneck pullover which usually meant they had been hired to wash floors somewhere or dish out food for the day at a cafeteria. The pullover covered his tattoos which made him otherwise virtually unemployable, attitudes being what they were. The boys were quite excited at Fred Dyer's idea of staging a friendly arm-wrestling contest between Orbit and Fred's friend and mine, Tommy Noakes. Though Orbit's feats of strength were well known, Tommy was an experienced brawler and had successfully arm-wrestled bigger men in the past. I wouldn't have put money on either one and saw no reason why a friendly contest wouldn't draw a small crowd, which for Fred Dyer would be the object of the exercise.

As we finished discussing the upcoming event and I got ready to go, I thrust my hands in my pockets and realized that I'd forgotten to give Tommy the book I'd found for him. I had a few minutes to spare so I walked back to the Boxing Club with Tommy's paperback copy of Michaela Denis's memoirs, *Leopard in My Lap*.

LONDON SKIN & BONES

I entered by the front door this time and there was the boy in the blue boxing gloves, still bouncing around the ring quite elegantly and looking as tempting as the last fondant in the box. Tommy was at the desk at the back and his eyes lit up at the sight of the book he'd been looking for. Tommy and I both remembered the old TV program *On Safari* featuring the big, gentle Belgian naturalist Armand Denis and his beautiful blonde wife Michaela, patiently stalking African and South American big game with their cameras and notebooks. Young Tommy had been smitten by the stunning Michaela and older Tommy expressed his thanks in little enthusiastic bursts of breath, each one containing a syllable and accompanied by a nod. I asked him about the proposed contest and he said yes, it was all set to happen in the old billiard room at the pub in a fortnight's time. Fred was even printing up flyers as though it was the Thriller in Manila. I headed out on my errand.

The following week was fairly uneventful, though at Boris's stamp shop, the Triplets, Elliot and Lionel, Boris's teenaged companions, launched with vigor into a new cooking course, regaling everyone with arcane details of the culinary art. The Triplets had seized on Fred Dyer's latest "special event," the arm-wrestling contest, to display their newly acquired culinary skills. The cooking lessons they were so enthusiastic about were officially known as "The Evelyn Grey Twenty Step World Cookery Course," something recommended to them by Miss Diamond, a little old lady who lived almost entirely on the largesse of the businesses she shamelessly puffed in her fortnightly column "I Recommend ...," easily the longest-running feature of the *Hampstead & Highgate Shoppers News*.

Miss Diamond had been in The Park to reassess the dubious delights of The Lorne Tea Shop (Seamus Moore called it The Forlorn Tea Shop), a faded, somewhat fusty establishment in the Finsbury Park High Street sporting starched, off-white tablecloths and specializing in "luncheonettes." The Lorne's windows were usually decorated with a range of dead bluebottles; its menu was distinguished by about half the listed items having their prices indicated by small, neatly-cut paper rectangles glued onto more ancient, and presumably more reasonable, amounts. Miss Diamond was almost certainly the only restaurant reviewer known to The Lorne and for all their shortcomings, she presented them with no challenge. Far from being anonymous, she was well known in the area, a dapper, gray-haired little figure, always dressed in one of her "costumes," a number of similar suits in pastel colors with matching shoes. And, as the name of her column suggested, words of criticism seldom encroached on her enthusiastic assessments. No matter how slatternly the service, how inadequate the fare or how squalid the ladies' lavatories, Miss Diamond was sure to find something nice to say about any establishment privileged to be included in her breezy roundups: "Newly extended Saturday hours should ensure this popular meeting place remains in vogue ..." Florence Diamond regarded The Lorne's dowdy, almost prewar ambience as a welcome oasis of refinement in the parched cultural terrain of Finsbury Park.

After her meal and note-taking at The Lorne, Miss Diamond dropped by the big back room of Boris's stamp shop to say hello and complain about some unseemly recent behavior on the part of "General Galtieri and his henchmen," the current Argentine military junta. In the course of her visit, the Triplets managed to divert her from her preoccupation with the South American situation by casually expressing an interest in cookery. This elicited from a raincoat pocket a much-folded illustrated periodical. Miss Diamond (neither her column nor anyone else ever used her first name) was an avid reader of *Woman* and *Women's Own,* two lookalike magazines for working and middle-class women that had been published forever and featured such female-friendly contributors as the chatty Beverley Nichols, the anodyne Godfrey Wynn, and an astrology column by someone called Gypsy Petulengro (apparently a portly, mustachioed stereotype complete with bandanna and earrings).

"Why not try this?" Miss Diamond ventured, smoothing out a slightly stained full-page advertisement for one of her old favorites. The proffered regimen was a book-and-correspondence culinary course outlining with near military precision a frontal attack on international cuisine in twenty apparently unalterable steps involving recipes "from the far corners of the Earth." The appeal of such dishes as Bulgarian fried cabbage stalks and *escargots aux* Solomon Islands found enthusiastic responses in the Triplets as they scrutinized and discussed the suggested prospectus. They quickly agreed to adopt The Evelyn Grey Twenty Step World Cookery Course, and thus become proficient in recreating the grub of all continents (Antarctica excepted). The following day they sent in their money (the course was not expensive) and were soon on their way.

Lionel had insisted that if he and Elliot were going to be accomplished chefs before the age of twenty, they must "do it *properly.*" If they were to work on the course together, Lionel insisted, they might, in his somewhat melodramatic phrase, be "swept away in a whirlpool of self-delusion." One of them, he suggested, should take the course and the other act as a disinterested and scrupulously impartial judge. Thus it came about that Elliot manhandled the pots and pans while Lionel hovered, claiming a gustatory *droit de seigneur* over each new dish, almost always pronouncing them "delicious!" or "a brilliant success!" This of course encouraged Elliot to even greater heights of culinary expertise *a la* Grey (who according to her cozy-looking ads was a beaming, bespectacled middle-aged woman in a smart cardigan, forever wielding a wooden spoon).

On the weekend of the big event, the designated *pièce de résistance* (Miss Gray was fluent in French) was Welsh Walnut and Leek Bread. Fred Dyer, the landlord of the Kings, was not the only one to express uncertainty that Welsh Walnut and Leek Bread would have much appeal for the locals, but both Triplets were firmly insistent that the Twenty Steps to World Cookery permitted no hedging, no deviation—and no substitutions. Miss Gray was nothing if not a harsh taskmistress. As no one seemed willing to press the point and Fred Dyer was understandably pleased with the prospect of a full house, the Four Kings' small but efficient baking oven was placed at the Triplets' disposal.

The Four Kings was crowded on the evening of the big event and as the arm-wrestling bout was announced, customers made their way into the old billiard room to take their places on oak benches and metal folding chairs. Fred announced the rules, pronouncing each word carefully in an unnecessarily loud voice. There were to be three rounds, the contestants seated, their forearms perpendicular, their hands locked in combat. If neither one had forced his opponent's hand to the tabletop by the sound of the bell that usually rang for "Time, gentlemen, please!" the round would be counted a draw. I sat at the back near the kitchen.

The first round ended quickly with Orbit the winner and it looked as though things might soon be over. In the second round, Tommy put up much more of a fight and people began glancing at the clock instead of staring at the contestants. With only a few seconds to go and all eyes on the bout or the time, the pub grew quiet. Suddenly, through the doorway beside me, Lionel came bouncing out of the kitchen loudly announcing "*The bread's ready!*"

This sudden interruption broke Orbit's concentration. Momentarily distracted, he turned toward the kitchen for an instant—and immediately his hand smacked onto the table, giving Tommy the round. Consternation and groaning from the assembled crowd was followed by a big cheer. Tommy and Orbit both looked sheepish. Fred Dyer kept things going as little slices of Lionel's walnut bread were handed round as though he had made them himself, and pronounced very tasty.

The third round lasted the distance. Thoroughly focused now, neither opponent would give way and at the bell the contest was duly pronounced a draw. The bar filled up as everyone ordered fresh drinks.

I was summoned to a spare seat by a burly, middle-aged man in army trousers and a Hawaiian shirt. It was my employer, the Old Sarge.

"Did you win anything?" I asked. Fred Dyer had deputized the more flirtatious of the barmaids to take bets.

"Sure!" Sarge replied, letting lose a rasping cough and unwrapping a cigar. "I bet on a draw!"

"Quite a long shot!" I ventured.

"I only bet long shots," said Sarge. "And never more than I could afford to wipe my arse on."

Tommy got pretty drunk that night. The Sarge assisted Seamus Moore in taking him home and tucking him in.

Orbit was very proud of the framed "Champion" certificate Fred Dyer had made up for each of the two contestants, and full of praise for his worthy opponent. "He's a nice man," he pronounced. "That bread and butter was really good!" When I thought about it, I remembered that we knew very well how easily distracted Orbit was. Boris's kitchen directive proved that. What we didn't know (but maybe Sarge did, he knew a lot of bits and pieces about everyone) was that Orbit, a quiet, friendly lad, also had a very poorly developed sense of competition.

An incidental but (for me) memorable feature of the Four Kings' arm-wrestling night was the presence of the boy in the blue boxing gloves. He had allowed someone to cut his hair—not to skinhead length but quite short, the blond quiff no longer able to fall onto his forehead. I tried to catch his eye but had no luck. I was able to point him out to Andy Boom, a skinhead friend who had the room next to mine in the Turle Road house, just before the boxing boy vanished quietly into the night.

A couple of weeks later Miss Diamond dropped by Boris's shop again, making a special trip to deliver a large handbag full of stamps, all neatly cut from envelope corners. The Triplets engaged her in spirited conversation on the merits of the Evelyn Grey Twenty Step World Cookery Course. By this time, the uneven division of labor between Elliot and Lionel had been abandoned and both Triplets were contributing to the making of various supposedly French sauces and South African curries.

"You know this picture in Evelyn Grey's ad?" Miss Diamond mused as she and the Triplets sipped tea at Boris's table. "She's not the same person as when I did my cookery course. Not the same at all. Her hair's different. And her face is not the same either."

"When did you take your course?" Lionel asked.

"Oh years ago—after the War though."

"Well, no *wonder!*" Elliot interrupted, "I expect they've gone through four or five Evelyn Greys since then."

"I *expect*," Lionel chimed in using his haughtiest manner, "there *is* or *was* no Evelyn Grey, she's a *mere* advertising *figment*, conjured up by an *image* consultant."

"Oh!" exclaimed Miss Diamond with a little giggle, perhaps unaccustomed to such knowing iconoclasm from one so young. "I suppose you may be right. And I wrote to her you know, to thank her for the course." She raised two bony fingers to her lips. "She wrote such a nice letter back too, with lovely handwriting. You don't see handwriting like that these days. I think I still have it somewhere."

On the way home, I ran into Andy, home early from an afternoon of carpet-laying. He was wearing baggy army pants, a tight black T-shirt and his ever-present Doc Martens. We talked about the contest and agreed it had been Orbit's big night.

"I wonder where Blue Boy went," I said as we headed home. I knew Andy fancied him too.

"He'll be back," he replied. "I can't remember his name—John something I think—but he's still on the books at the Boxing Club." Andy jumped up onto the low brick wall at the corner of our street and walked along it, his arms outstretched, one foot in front of the other like a tightrope walker. "He should be a *skin!*" he shouted, clenching his fists and raising his arms over his head.

"You think?"

"Yeah, I want to shave his crotch!" He jumped off the wall, grinned, gave me a little dig in the ribs, and blew air through his pursed lips with a little "phtt." Then he did his rubber-leg dance along the curb until we reached the gate. He flipped the latch and pulled one of his funny faces. As we headed inside, I thought how handsome and sexy he was with his cropped head and his beautiful long eyelashes.

IN MY DREAMS I CAN DRIVE

There was not much to do in our part of London after dark. The shops were shut. Ali's caff was shut. The Four Kings, like every other pub in London, called "Time, Ladies and Gentlemen, Please!" at 11 PM. Some of us got together in the back of Boris Mostoyenko's stamp shop, but on the way home, the streets were dark and lonely. After midnight, the only possibility of finding something to eat and a little company lay a fifteen-minute walk to the north—the Roundhouse.

The Roundhouse had once been a stylish garage in the Art Deco style but during the War had fallen into desuetude and never really recovered. It had gone through a number of owners over the years and when we discovered it, its coffee urn, mismatched tables and chairs, and single remaining petrol pump served as a sometime social center for passing motorbikers. Some of our local skinhead contingent found their way there from time to time, and often left in the company of friendly leatherboys. But the Roundhouse never kept regular hours, and was often closed at night. It was still worth a visit though, if you were feeling up to a walk, as the small asphalt plaza in front of the building was a frequent stopping point for Tommy Noakes's chip wagon.

Tommy had a number of regular stops, most of them near factories and other sites where people worked at night. Tommy, a journeyman fighter from the local boxing club, drove around at night serving tea, chips, gravy, pickled onions, and hardboiled eggs at his selected locations. As with the Roundhouse itself, his hours were irregular, so you took your chances.

LONDON SKIN & BONES

It was a cool night in early spring when I ran into Emmanuel Litvinauer and heard his story. I was restless and couldn't sleep. I had been having a series of vivid dreams—dreams about unknown streets, squares and laneways, long, empty roads that passed through devastated building sites and empty lots. I had never learned to drive but in my dreams I seemed to be driving an old American car like the succession of low-slung Hudsons, Studebakers, and Kaisers my Uncle Bob used to drive around Detroit. I always drove very slowly, hugging the curb. At some point, I began to realize that the fragments of cityscape I encountered in my dreams were linked to each other, that they were all part of one city—not a romantic dream city but a rather bleak, half-abandoned place, where discarded papers blew through streets and squares that were eerily quiet. The dreams were not frightening or disturbing, just odd. I started to wonder where I was I driving to, or what I was looking for. But that night I couldn't sleep, and decided to go for a walk.

I put on my tweed overcoat, slung my camera bag over my shoulder, and headed out, leaving a note for my friend Andy, whose room was next to mine on the top floor of the rooming house on Turle Road, in case he wanted to sleep in my double bed as he often did. "Gone for a walk, back soon."

A light rain had fallen earlier and the swish, swish of the tires from the few cars passing on the Holloway Road felt oddly comforting in the otherwise lonely, slightly misty night. I chose the Roundhouse that night for no particular reason other than that it was somewhere to walk to, and better than wandering aimlessly which is always depressing. But as I approached, I was glad to see the rectangle of light from the chip wagon and hear the faint reggae tune emanating from Tommy's radio.

A burly good-natured soul, Tommy could occasionally be quite animated but most of the time said little more than a few words. He greeted me with a broad, toothless grin and the suggestion of a cup of tea. I eagerly accepted and dug into my pocket for change.

"Very quiet tonight," he said, which wasn't surprising as it was quiet every night.

"Sarge has those Navy pullovers you wanted," I told him. (I worked in the local military surplus shop.)

"Ooh, goody, I'll come by tomorrow."

As I stood exchanging small talk with Tommy and drinking my tea, I noticed someone had abandoned a rather handsome dining chair of blond polished wood, its seat missing, now half sunk into a deep puddle. With two of its legs in the mucky water, it looked oddly out of place against the rough black tarmac. I snapped a few photos, partly to test some new film stock I'd acquired and try out different exposures. As I was putting my camera away, an elderly bald man with a muscular build and a slight paunch came ambling toward us.

"Ooh, look now, who's coming?" asked Tommy in his eager, breathy half-stammer.

I had met Emmanuel Litvinauer a few times at Boris Mostoyenko's shop. Like many of Boris's regulars, he had some sort of East European connection, regularly dropping off copies of a mimeographed newsletter called *Transnistrian Bylines*. This obscure and rather blotchy production he sold here and there and dutifully mailed to various embassies and literary figures, hoping for subscriptions or commendations. Most recipients, he readily admitted, ignored him, but he had received encouraging replies from three of the names on his list: "That excellent publication, *Transnistrian Bylines* ..."—Lawrence Durrell. "Amazing!"—Colin Wilson. "Keep up the good work!"—Roger Baker. These kind words, highlighted in little boxes, were routinely quoted in rotation, in different issues.

I knew also that Manny Litvinauer helped old Mrs. Cricheloe feed the stray cats in the local churchyard. He liked to pass out boiled sweets and had once given me a copy of the first edition of a fascinating book, Siegfried Krackauer's *From Caligari to Hitler: A Psychological History of German Film*.

Squinting, twitching, and chain-smoking, Litvinauer—like so many of the immigrants and refugees who dropped by the stamp shop—loved to talk. Which meant, of course, that he loved to find someone who would listen. I knew I'd be listening for a bit that night. Litvinauer bought a styrofoam cup of tea and a box of chips and gravy and joined me sitting on the low, concrete-topped brick wall that ran around the perimeter of the Roundhouse yard and provided the only available seating. I remember thinking how Litvinauer's only slightly accented English differed from the heavily inflected speech of many of Boris's European acquaintances.

"I couldn't sleep," he told me.

"I couldn't sleep either," I said.

"I left my car around in the back streets by that little park where I used to take my dog—but that was years ago, that good old dog's been gone for

LONDON SKIN & BONES

five years now, I really should get another dog, it's good to walk a dog at night, gives you some reason to be out, you know what I mean?"

"Yes," I said. "I sometimes walk Sarge's dog Soldier. You meet other people with dogs and you can talk dogs with them."

"I'm on my own now," Litvinauer confided. "My wife, she's gone. We have no children."

Litvinauer sipped his tea and stuck a plastic fork into his chips and gravy. "Boris speaks very highly of you," he said, his voice almost a whisper. "He says you can be trusted with a confidence."

"I don't spread things around if they're private," I admitted.

"Yes, yes, that's good. You know I haven't slept well for weeks and I have to tell somebody what happened. I was going to tell the vicar, you know, at the church, nice man, but somehow I just couldn't. Not at the time. But I have to get it off my chest, you don't mind?"

What could I say?

Between sips of tea and mouthfuls of chips, Emmanuel Litvinauer confessed his greatest and most recent sin. He had, so he said, killed a man.

"I don't sleep well," he repeated, "not since my wife died. Well, not for a long time really. I drove the car to Regents Park and thought I'd have a walk by the canal."

I knew that last remaining fragment of the old barge canal that began at the top end of Regents Park and continued around the park and as far as St. John's Wood. Part of it had grassy banks with trees and a pleasant little path overlooked by old ivy-covered houses.

"There was a full moon and it was very pleasant down by the canal," Litvinauer recalled. "Very pleasant." As he sipped his coffee I noticed how his fingers and little blond mustache were badly stained with nicotine. He had large, liquid eyes that fixed you in a pale stare.

"I used to walk the old dog there years ago. Very seldom ran into anyone. And that night too, it was quite deserted, quite deserted. But I'd only been walking a couple of minutes when this man comes walking slowly toward me. As he passed me, I saw his face. I saw it very clearly and it gave me a terrible shock." As he spoke, reggae music from Tommy's radio filtered across the Roundhouse yard in the darkness.

"You know," Litvinauer confided, "sometimes you see a face and you *know* who it is. You *know*—even if it's been years. You never forget that face!

And that's what happened that night. I was surprised. I was *frightened*! But I had no doubt."

At this point, Manny finished his chips and asked me to wait while he fetched something from his car. "I'll bring the car round. I want to show you. I'll drive you home." And off he went, leaving me sitting on the parapet, which, even insulated as I was by my tweed coat, was cold and beginning to be uncomfortable. I watched him head off into the night and then strolled over to Tommy's chip wagon.

Tommy, I noticed, had put his partial plate in and displayed a full range of gleaming choppers.

"Them pullovers," he said. "Have they got the leather patches on the shoulders?"

"Yes, I think so."

"Ooh, goody. Manny go home?"

"No, he's coming back," I said. "Wants me to wait for him."

"Tosh!" said Tommy.

"What?"

"Peter Tosh on the tape. Lovely." And we listened together quietly, Tommy standing in the chip wagon, me leaning on the narrow counter, nobody else about.

Litvinauer soon pulled his little maroon car up to the curb and climbed out, holding a big book bulging with papers.

We sat together on the wall, our cups of tea steaming beside us.

Manny's book was a big, battered scrapbook stuffed with photographs, documents, and envelopes full of clippings. He began to leaf through it.

"You know," he said quietly, "all my family died in the camps. I still have nightmares about the camps. Nightmares about getting away. I dream about getting in a car and driving away—driving, driving, driving, away from the camp ... Ah, here it is." He unfolded an old magazine printed in a language I didn't recognize. It might have been Romanian. He turned to a photo on an inside page. It showed a group of uniformed prisoners standing behind a barbed wire fence. They looked impassive and resigned, except for one man who held out his hands as though pushing something away from him. On the near side of the wire were some German soldiers and two men in civilian dress, one middle-aged, the other very young.

"This is one of the camps my relatives were in," said Manny. He paused, and took a sip of tea. "This man here," he jabbed a yellowed finger at the image of the older man. "This man here—that is Doktor Friederich Lösener. A chemist, supposedly. Well, God knows what he was up to inspecting concentration camps, I don't like to think. They selected people, you know, for experiments. Maybe he wanted to test his chemicals, I don't know. But there he is. After the war he was tried and imprisoned for a while. I think he had a relative who helped save some half-Jews, but this one never did anything to help anyone but himself. They released him for poor health and he died soon afterwards. But ... you see this other man with him, the young man. The caption gives *no* name for him. But"—Manny looked me in the face and adopted a stage whisper—"I know who he is!"

Manny pulled his scarf around his throat. "I came face to face with him! Imagine, after all these years—and here in London! I was walking by the Regents Park canal. It was dark, there was a bit of a moon. Bright moon. No one about. Then I saw this bloke—bloke in a gray overcoat, walking beside the canal towards me. He seemed lost in his thoughts, didn't see me til he was right on me. But I saw him, got a good look at his face. I couldn't forget that face, I'd seen it so many times in the picture, it was Lösener's assistant—over thirty years older, of course, but it was him all right, there was no doubt.

"We were almost as close as I am to you now. And I looked him right in the face—that pale, expressionless face. As he looked into my eyes he must have seen something there he didn't like because he suddenly turned on his heel and started to walk quickly back the way he'd come.

"I felt so strange," Manny said, "as though I was two different people. My body was running after the man in the overcoat but I was right there watching—watching everything that was going on—and I couldn't stop myself."

Manny looked around as if he wanted to make sure there was no one else there. But we were alone, with not even a car passing. Only Tommy's chip wagon a few yards away in the Roundhouse yard, the reggae music playing softly on the radio.

"I caught up with him and was going to take hold of him but he turned around and faced me. I flung my hands out in front of me"—Manny gestured and spilled a little of his tea onto the gravel at the side of the road. "He moved backwards and slipped in the mud. He fell over and got up onto his knees, and I reached out to him. You know, I don't know whether I was trying to help him up or give him a push. But I never got the chance. His feet slipped out from under him and he was into the canal before I knew what was happening. He reached out for the stone parapet but his hands just slipped down the wall and he was gone—into the water with hardly a sound. I thought he would come to the surface but he didn't. He couldn't have sunk, could he? Not that quickly! He must have been carried away somehow. Oh, I was so frightened! I knew I'd killed him. I can't swim, you know," he added.

"I stood there by the canal. It had all happened so quickly. I didn't know what to do. I couldn't have saved him, even if I'd wanted to. It was dark. I looked for him but the water was so black. I didn't mean to kill him. But if it wasn't for me, he'd still be alive."

Manny took a swig of tea and looked out toward the road. My thoughts tumbled through my mind. He had killed a man. But all he had done was to chase the man for a few yards and witness his apparent death. He was obviously upset and still quite frightened.

"Did you tell the police?" I heard myself say, thinking it a stupid question.

Manny was quiet for a moment. "I wasn't going to. All I wanted to do was to get out of there and go home and try to forget what happened. I was sweating and my heart was racing. I walked a few feet along to that little path that leads from the canal back up to the street. And when I came around the corner I got the fright of my life—well, *two* frights in one night! There was a man there on the street. A young man, lighting a cigarette. I'll never forget his face as he glanced at me. God knows what I must have looked like, I was frightened to death. But I managed to walk down the street and when I looked back, he was gone. Then I knew I must tell the police so I used a call box and phoned them. I told them I'd seen a man fall into the Regents Park canal. And then it started to pour with rain and I went home."

I opened my mouth to say something but Manny spoke first. "For the next week," he said, "I was so bloody frightened. I stayed in my apartment. I thought the police would come knocking on my door at any minute! Finally, I had to go out to get groceries and I picked up a paper and the *Hampstead & Highgate Shoppers News.*"

Manny crumpled up his styrofoam cup, turned around, and tossed it across the yard, hitting the inside of Tommy's plastic rubbish bin like an expert basketball player. He rummaged through his thick pile of papers and produced a newspaper clipping, a photograph with the headline "Funeral of Local Businessman" and a caption. The photo showed an elderly woman dressed in black and several other people standing in the Highgate Cemetery. The caption indicated simply that the funeral of Paul Hahn, a German-born importer and longtime resident of Hampstead, had taken place a few days earlier. Such items, whether of funerals, weddings, lost dogs or announcements of church bazaars or yoga classes, were the paper's standard fare. No other information was provided. But Manny Litvinauer circled one particular face with his finger.

"*That's* the young man!" he said, looking me in the face. "That's the one I saw. He saw me running away from the canal. If he identifies me, I'm a goner. Oh dear, should I just kill myself?"

"Manny, you've done nothing wrong," I assured him, questioning myself as I said it. "Things aren't that bad."

Up to that point, I had been shocked by what Manny Litvinauer had said. But I felt no real stake in it. Manny, though he had confided in me for some reason of his own, was not someone I knew well. I was just the recipient of a rather confused confession. The commonplace photograph of the funeral group changed all that, and suddenly dragged me by the heart into Manny's peculiar story.

The well-dressed young man in the photo, standing next to the elderly woman in the old-fashioned veil, was someone I knew, a sometime friend by the name of Farouk Wylie. I had last seen Farouk before he had left London for Paris, apparently accompanied by a man his mother had married. Now here he was—back in London, looking suave and self-possessed as ever, on the elbow of Paul Hahn's veiled widow!

I excused myself—"I have to take a piss"—and walked over to the pile of oil drums and machine parts behind the Roundhouse. I pissed discreetly into a half-hidden clump of bushes and went back to the chip wagon.

"You all right?" asked Tommy.

"Yes, I'll be all right, Manny just gave me a bit of a shock."

"Ooh, you need this," was Tommy's immediate response. He reached under the counter and brought out a little bottle labeled Rescue Remedy. "Put a few drops of this under your tongue." I did as he said. "And have another cup of tea."

I thanked Tommy, paid for the tea and walked back to Manny. By this time he had left our perch on the wall and was sitting in his car. His papers were on the back seat.

"Come on in and get warm," he said. "I've turned the heater on. Here, you sit here, the steering wheel will get in my way."

It was good to warm up and as we sat there together Manny fell silent. I sat behind the wheel. Manny sat in the passenger seat beside me and spread his papers and the pages of his big book in front of him.

"Do you drive?" Manny asked.

"No. I never learned," I said. "In my dreams I can drive," I found myself telling him.

Suddenly Manny perked up and looked me square in the face.

"*I* learned to drive in my dreams!" he said. "I *knew* we were fellow spirits!"

"How did *that* happen?" I asked.

"*Tapes!*" he explained. "I bought these tapes. You can learn while you're sleeping. Driving is easy. Here, you can learn in a few minutes. Here, release the brake and drive around the Roundhouse yard."

I looked through the window of the car and watched the light in the back of the chip wagon go out and the headlights come on. Tommy was closing up for the night and preparing to drive away.

Sitting oddly behind the wheel in the stuffy car, the strangeness of the night's goings-on suddenly hit me. Here was this peculiar man who imagined he had learned to drive in his sleep and whose actions had led to a man's death, urging me to drive a car for the first time in my life, without a single lesson! Emmanuel Litvinauer was breathlessly explaining to me the workings of the car, its various levers and pedals, and I realized quite suddenly that I wanted very much to go home. Manny's bulging eyes, moist lips and mousy blond mustache suddenly made him seem disturbed, almost repellent. I turned the door handle and got out of the car. I felt slightly unsteady on my feet but the night's cold felt refreshing.

"Manny," I told him as he slid over into the driver's seat, "if I try to drive this car, I'm likely to run it into the wall." Manny nodded. "And I think you have two choices. You can either go to the police—or you can sit tight. Just don't tell any lies."

Manny nodded again, suddenly subdued. "Do you mind walking home?" he asked. "I think I want to sit here a while."

I told him I'd enjoy the walk. He thanked me for listening to his story. It made him feel better, he said. Feeling sorry for him I told him we'd talk again and I headed down the road, leaving him sitting in his little car.

The next evening after work I headed to Boris Mostoyenko's stamp shop before dinner. Boris was alone, dressed in his usual flannels and cardigan, with a cigarette in his mouth, washing up at the kitchen sink at the back of the shop. I sat at the big round table and asked him about Emmanuel Litvinauer. "Was he in the camps?"

"Manny? No. His family were Jews from Transnistria, between Romania and the Ukraine. He was evacuated from somewhere in Europe just before the war. I think he was interned for a while. But he was lucky. All his family perished in the camps. He was called up later in the war but I don't think he saw action. Maybe he got as far as Gibraltar."

"He told me some strange stories," I said.

"He's a bit of a fantasist. He's been in and out of the Rest Home, you know."

A fantasist! Could he have made up the whole thing? I wondered. I went over to the magazine pile to rummage through the stamp magazines and copies of *Mister* and *Gay News*. I found the back issue of the *Shoppers News* with the photo of the funeral, and wondered whether I'd ever hear from Farouk Wylie again.

The wet, cold days and nights fell away early that year and gave way to a warm, sunny spring. I spent weekends visiting my friends near Chipping Ongar and walking in Epping Forest. During the week, I worked for the Old Sarge in his military surplus shop. Manny 's tale of his harrowing evening by the canal soon faded from consciousness. Then one afternoon as I was helping Sarge sort and size a load of Yugoslavian army pants, a phone call came through for me. It was Farouk Wylie.

"I've missed you!" he purred in his sinuous, sexy voice. Farouk, I knew very well, was an accomplished seducer. Women and men alike, even straight men, succumbed to his charms. Dark and handsome with pointed eyes, smooth skin suggestive of coffee and olives, and usually immaculately—and expensively—dressed, he was always able to make you feel *you* were sexy, interesting, and attractive. His manner always seemed to suggest that you and he were involved in some intimate, secret plot that the rest of the world knew nothing about. In bed, he was enthusiastic and versatile. He smoked too much and sometimes his breath was redolent of tobacco. But he was hard to resist.

"I just got back from Paris," he said, as he might have said, I'm just back from shopping. "Come and visit me."

"Where are you?"

"I'm in Exeter!"

I had spent some time in Exeter a few years before. It had been heavily bombed during the War and the new, modern buildings had been built to fit in well with the plan of the old town, its ancient stone walls and narrow lanes. My grandfather used to live there.

"I don't know a soul here," Farouk added, a claim I found hard to believe as his effortless charm easily found him companions. "Come keep me company."

My friend Paul was short of money and had been asking to fill in at Sarge's shop for a while so I could easily get away. I could make arrangements to visit Exeter the next week.

"Are you still seeing that skinhead boyfriend of yours?"

"Andy Boom. I am."

"Bring him along if you think it would be fun."

"I think it would, I said. If he can get away from his job."

"What does he do?" Farouk asked.

"He lays carpets and installs flooring."

"Well, bring him along and we can have a party! Do you think he'll shove his bare arse in my face?"

"I wouldn't be at all surprised."

"I can't wait. Let me know when you're arriving. There's lots to drink and smoke."

"You can tell us all about Paris," I suggested.

"Paris is a bore," he said and hung up.

I always felt comfortable in Exeter. Since visiting there as a boy, it had been one of my favorite places in England, a small Devonian city on a very human, walkable scale with a famous cathedral, good cafés and bookshops, and a steady influx of European students and shoppers.

It was late at night. Farouk Wylie was living in a rather grand furnished flat over a bicycle shop near the town center. He lounged, knees up, legs apart, on a black Swedish modern couch laden with cushions. One wall of the flat was filled with high bookcases but apart from a few paperback mysteries and a set of wine glasses, they were empty. Farouk was flipping his cigarette ashes into a polished metal ashtray perched on his lap.

"The people who own this flat are in the middle of moving in—or out— or something," he said, blowing smoke into the air. "They're in Majorca. I

"We were all three contented, after an enjoyable evening"

only have a couple of months here. We must be careful not to burn holes in the furniture." He wore a pair of tight blue underpants and high, nylon socks held up with old-fashioned garters. I had never seen anyone wear such an item before and couldn't decide whether they were sexy or amusing, or both. Shirtless in Doc Martens and jeans, his braces beneath him, Andy was sitting nearby in an overstuffed arm chair, nodding rhythmically under Farouk's headphones, staring across the room, a little smile on his face, oblivious to everything but the music. We were all quite contented after an enjoyable evening of sex, music, and takeaway Chinese food. I came in from the bathroom. Under my bare feet, the brightly colored woolen carpets felt warm and soft. Bottles, magazines, and a small baggie of grass littered the glass and chrome coffeetable. A few records lay on the floor. Farouk raised his voice and turned toward Andy.

"I think frequent, violent orgasms are essential for good health, don't you?"

But Andy, still under headphones and eating spaghetti out of a tin, remained oblivious.

"What's he listening to anyway?"

"Bluegrass," I said.

Farouk pursed his lips. "I loved yew / so I killed yew / so now they're going to hang me / down by the riversaahd."

"Something like that."

Farouk leaned over to me. "He's wonderful!" he whispered in my ear. "Dining habits are a bit odd though," he added, raising one eyebrow in his best Dirk Bogarde manner.

I decided to ask Farouk what had taken him to Paris.

"My mother's husband," he answered. "He took rather a fancy to me." He turned and looked at me with a little smile. Since I had last seen him, he had grown a thin pencil mustache. "Does it make me look like a gigolo?" he had asked. At that moment, he just looked handsome, his hair for once not immaculately groomed, his garters drawing attention to themselves. "But we ... had a falling out. But I got a position with a German gentleman, a perfumier."

"Paul Hahn," I blurted without thinking.

"Aren't you *clever*, you do surprise me," replied Farouk, who didn't seem at all surprised. "Did you know Paul?"

"I saw the notice of his funeral in a local paper," I said.

LONDON SKIN & BONES

"Oh, *The Highhorse Shopper's Wank!*"

"That's the one."

"Not a very good photo of me," he sighed.

Now or never, I thought.

"How did he die?"

"Well, *actually*," Farouk drawled, "he fell into the Regents Park canal. I know that sounds funny but that's what happened. He was an odd bloke, neurotic, very closeted, very mysterious. Lots of money. He owned a perfume factory and imported perfumes and cosmetics from Europe into England. Austrian he was."

Farouk sat up, set the ashtray on the coffeetable, and began to roll one of his exquisitely thin joints.

"I was hired as his private secretary but there really wasn't much for me to do. I think the old boy wanted company more than anything. He'd been in the War, you know, and I think he saw things there that he didn't want to remember. He was decent to me." I wondered whether sexual services had been among the terms of employment.

"There wasn't much paperwork to do. The most difficult thing really was fending off calls from his sister who was a prying old biddy who wouldn't leave him alone. I'd often accompany him out to dinners—we ate very well, I must say—and for walks. He liked to take walks. We were at his maisonette in London when he died." He flashed me a glance. "He was a strange bloke. We'd be walking in a park or somewhere and he'd tell me to wait for him. I'd sit on a bench or hang about for a while and he'd wander off by himself for twenty minutes or a half hour. He'd come back and we'd finish the walk. He seemed very lonely. Very sad."

"You weren't with him when he died?"

"No, he told me to stay in that night. They fished his body out of the canal the next morning. Coroner's inquest said it was an accident. I was shocked, of course. Even more so when I heard he'd left me some money. Most of his estate went to his sister who was quite distraught, poor thing." Farouk lit the joint, took a drag, and instead of handing it to me, came over and placed it between my lips. He stood in front of me and ran his hands through his slick, black hair. His smooth chest and surprisingly bushy armpits were redolent of patchouli and—was it cloves?

I looped my fingers into the waistband of his powder blue undershorts. "You didn't follow him?"

107

Farouk raised his eyebrows. His dark eyes seemed more hooded than ever and he flashed a smile. "You probably think I bumped the old boy off! You *are* wicked! Well, I didn't. I don't think the old boy bumped himself off either. He wouldn't have thrown himself into a canal. He had a gun. He would have shot himself. I think the poor old sod just had one swig too many from that flask he kept on him, got lost in the dark, and pitched into the drink."

"What are you going to do now?" I asked.

"There's a nice old lady up the street wants me to help her with her flower shop. I think I will."

"Going to lie low for a while?"

"I think so." What was left of the joint had gone out and I rested it on the coffeetable ashtray. Farouk smiled and looked down at me, about to say something, as I sat on the couch in front of him. But at that point, his proximity had become too enticing and whatever his topic of conversation might have been, it would have to wait.

Over the next few weeks I wondered if Manny might drop by the stamp shop, though I wasn't sure what I might say to him. One evening, I was sitting with Boris at the big table at the back of the shop, sorting through bags of a big on-paper Mission Mixture, wondering if I should tell him the whole story. Was Farouk Wylie actually there the night Paul Hahn drowned? Had he lied to me? Or could Manny have imagined him? But Manny's confession had been in confidence, so I confined myself to asking Boris about mysteries in general—those events in one's life that contradict one another or that you're suspicious of or that just don't add up.

That was when Boris told me the story of his friend's mother's gardening prize. This friend, it seemed, did not get on particularly well with his mother, a vain and secretive woman who judged local flower and vegetable shows. But she had a number of talents that she was always boasting about. In her youth, she said (she was referring to that blessed time Before the War) she had been an *expert* gardener, one of the best in the country. She was particularly proud of winning First Prize in an All-County Garden Fair. "Who knows what I could have done if the War hadn't come along!"

Boris's friend, the story went, thought his mother's boasting tiresome and found it odd that he had never seen any evidence of Mother's spectacular win. So one day when the mother was out, Boris's friend went into her room and rummaged around in her papers. At this point, Boris flashed me his

"That wasn't very nice" look over his spectacles, the pair he called his "Leon Trotsky specials."

"So," I asked, "did she really not win the big prize?"

"Oh, yes, she won the prize all right. But—*she wasn't his mother*." Here Boris adopted a stage whisper. "That's why I don't read other people's correspondence," he said. "*Because I don't want to know what's written there!*"

The next few weeks were busy ones at work as many lots of surplus goods all came in at once. But the days with Sarge were not long and always congenial, and my weekends were my own to explore London as I wished. One of my Saturday morning pleasures was riding on the top of the double-decker bus that traveled from Ilford down through the East End, all the way to Tottenham Court Road. The bus stand near the Ilford traffic circle is the beginning of the trip so I could usually manage to sit on my preferred seat, at the front of the upper deck. I loved the long journey winding through the streets and lanes with a bird's eye view of the street markets, the barrow-boys and used goods stalls, the cloth merchants and junk dealers and vegetable sellers and crowds of shopping families. I never tired of it.

Sometimes on these trips Andy or another friend would come with me, but on that particular Saturday, I was by myself. I had paid for my ticket, I had a few Pounds in my pocket, and I was heading to the bookshops around Charing Cross Road, looking forward to an afternoon of browsing and book buying. I had arranged to meet my friend Oswell Blakeston and his partner the painter Max Chapman for dinner in the evening.

The bus had stopped briefly in traffic somewhere around Mile End. A café of the sort frequented by working men had a few nondescript tables and chairs on an adjoining laneway. From my top-of-the-bus perch I recognized of all people—it was an unlikely setting for him—Farouk Wylie, who had dropped off the radar again as he did from time to time. He was sitting with another man at one of the small tables. Then just as the bus started up again, I realized—or thought I realized—that the other man was Manny.

The bus lurched off and though I craned my neck to see, the café with its pavement tables and half-hidden laneway vanished from view, leaving me with a sudden rush of half-formed questions.

Should I get off the bus and go back, I wondered, just to see if they were still there? And what if they were? Or should I just sit back, continue the journey, and look forward to what promised to be a very nice weekend? One

IAN YOUNG

can face such dilemmas, sitting on top of a London bus on a sunny Saturday afternoon!

As it happened, my photo of the designer chair sunk into the mud-puddle caught the eye of Windom Price, editor of the *Hampstead & Highgate Shoppers News*, who said he would like to print it in his paper. This surprised me; the photo, though well-exposed, was perfectly ordinary, hardly the arty study I had intended. But a week later I was presented with a small check. Windom Price was quite ceremonial about it as though bestowing some obscure Papal order. I found my picture printed on Page 7 under the headline "Potholes: What Can Be Done?" I added it to my list of publications. The money came in very handy.

For months afterwards, I would dream about driving slowly through the silent, unknown city in the big, low-slung American car with the left-hand drive.

SEXUAL ALTERNATIVES FOR MEN

"Lionel has bunny feet!"

It was early morning—unusually early for me to be sitting at the big table at the back of Boris Mostayenko's stamp shop, drinking tea, but I had been alerted that Farouk Wylie, a friend who was often good for surprises, would be dropping by—"I can't stop for long!"—with a valise of books for me.

I used my key to let myself in and as I made tea, Elliot, the elder of the Triplets (by several minutes), came down from the flat they shared with Boris above the shop. As the kettle whistled, brother Lionel, still in pajamas, crept downstairs to join us and stood at the bottom of the steps, rubbing his eyes, his woolen socks concertinaed around his ankles and protruding in rabbit-like extensions along the floorboards.

"Lionel has bunny feet!" Elliot muttered, pointing and nodding sagely. Lionel hiked his socks up.

"Why is everyone up so early?" he asked.

"Delivery," explained Elliot, as Lionel went to the sink and splashed water on his face.

The two were identical brothers in their late teens, boyishly good looking with fair skin, rosy cheeks, and luxuriant black hair. Most identical twins can be told apart by the keen eye, but Elliot and Lionel were so identical that without a good view of a tiny gap between two upper front teeth, only slightly wider than a hair—Elliot's gap being just a fraction further apart than Lionel's—no one (except Boris) could tell one from the other.

"Farouk says he has a case of books for me," I said. Lionel, not wanting to be seen in his dishevelled state by so suave and handsome a visitor as Farouk, headed back upstairs to change, emerging a few minutes later in a bright yellow shirt, tight bondage pants (the latest vogue, cross-gartered with many buckles and zippers), and the same unruly socks. We were all drinking tea when the doorbell rang.

Farouk Wylie was half Egyptian, with a lithe body, almond eyes, silky skin the color of caramel and an intimate, confiding manner that charmed—and often seduced—acquaintances of both sexes. He was wearing an expensive camel-hair coat over a dark suit and silk tie. He threw his arm over my shoulder and kissed me on the mouth. He was accompanied by a large black valise which Lionel hauled past the various scavenged items at the front of the shop, handing it over to Elliot who parked it against the pillar of the table where it sat expectantly, like the bomb in Hitler's bunker.

"How are you, chaps?" asked Farouk, lighting one of his Egyptian cigarettes with a kitchen match. The Triplets avowed that they were in top form, all ready for the new day ahead. Farouk lounged on the couch blowing smoke but declined the offer of a cup of tea.

"Don't be a stranger," he muttered, clasping my hand and pulling me gently onto the couch next to him. "How's our friend Andy?" he whispered. He turned toward the Triplets and raised his voice a little: "I expect you know the very dishy proletarian roommate?" Farouk was referring to Andy Boom, housemate, skinhead, installer of industrial carpeting and self-declared "bugger."

"He's fine," I assured him, "though he's not actually my roommate. He has the room *beside* mine."

"Separate bedrooms, always so wise." pronounced Farouk, extracting a flake of tobacco from between his lips with a fingernail. "I'd love to pop round, just the two of us, and join him for a pot of tea *in his room* but I'm in a hurry today. I did some deliveries for a chap called Barrington, and he was a bit short of cash, couldn't pay me—so he gave me these books and this very smart briefcase instead. You'll know what to do with them." He slipped a small brass key into my hand, got up from the couch, and approached the blackboard fixed to the wall beside the stove. A chalked message read CLEAN SOCKS ARE IMPORTANT. Farouk shot me a glance.

"Finsbury Park has so much wisdom. Is that why you live here?"

"I live here," I iterated, trying not to sound defensive, "because I was told it's the cheapest district in London that isn't actually dangerous."

LONDON SKIN & BONES

At that point, a car horn sounded in the street. "There's my ride!" said Farouk, extinguishing his cigarette. "Sorry to run off so quickly, I'd love to stay and keep you all company"—he flashed an appreciative glance at the Triplets—"but duty calls."

I escorted Farouk to the door with both Triplets following close behind in their stocking feet. A gray Bentley had pulled up in front of the shop and a silver-haired, pink-skinned chauffeur of indeterminate age wearing a smart uniform hopped out and opened the back door. Farouk slid into the spacious, leather-upholstered back seat and waved from the open window as we stood on the step. "I'll phone you soon!" he called.

"Promises, promises!" I replied, grinning as I said it.

"Kiss Andy's arse for me!" As the Bentley whisked Farouk Wylie away, waving to us like royalty, the Triplets whispered and giggled to themselves.

"Be still my heart!" one of them intoned.

"Is that his car?" asked the other. I shook my head, wondering whose car it was, and what sort of deliveries he might have been making for the fellow Barrington. "He has such fine bones! Like Lauren Bacall." He was quite right, I realized, and Farouk's familiar Dirk Bogarde look, economically effected with just one eyebrow and a corner of the mouth, would never seem quite the same again.

"Next time he comes around we must get him in the beanbag chair!" Elliot said thoughtfully. The beanbag chair was one of the oddly varied array of furnishings in the Triplets' upstairs flat. "You're quite helpless in a beanbag chair!" he explained, making it sound like a torture device.

"Especially," I suggested, "if you have a couple of boys on top of you!"

"Boris says you have a special job today," said one of the Triplets as I checked my watch against the bus schedule pinned to the notice board.

And special it was. I had spent several weekends cataloguing the library of Boris's old friend Marcus, a job I had been able to do in considerable comfort. Marcus Aurelius Grumbacher was a coin dealer and evaluator, a property speculator, and an old and intimate friend of Boris's, and his Georgian-style home and business headquarters in Hampstead housed an intriguing collection of numismatic literature. As my modest bibliographical abilities had apparently proved satisfactory, Marcus had recommended me to his near neighbor, an eccentric Liberal peer bearing the august title of Lord Piltdown of Bath and the Wash. Marcus had made it clear that he, not his Lordship, would be paying me for the job—an arrangement that

IAN YOUNG

was fine with me as I knew Marcus to be a generous—even extravagantly generous—employer.

"I mustn't be late," I mused. "Farouk isn't the only one to travel in exalted circles. You'll be impressed to learn that I'm cataloguing a library for a peer of the realm! I start today." I knew the Triplets were fascinated by all things royal and aristocratic, and indeed they were all ears.

"Who is it? Who is it?" asked Lionel.

"Yes, tell us!" Elliot chimed in. "I bet it's Screaming Lord Sutch!"

"Screaming Lord Sutch isn't actually a lord," I said pedantically. "He's just a mad musician who tries to get himself elected. If he were a *real* lord," I added, "he couldn't sit in the Commons, he'd have to renounce the title he awarded himself." I realized this wasn't very clear but the boys had lost interest in the distinguished founder of the National Teenage Party.

"Are you going to tell us who it is?"

"It's one of Marcus's Hampstead neighbors, Lord Piltdown."

My mention of the name elicited little hoots and snorts and cries of "Oh my *dear!*" from the boys.

"Oh, it's old *Piltdown!*" exclaimed Elliot. "Find that paper with one of his ads! He has an ad in *Gay News* looking for a boyfriend every month, regular as clockwork." Lionel rummaged around in the pile of papers and magazines that always occupied a straight-back chair in a corner of the kitchen. The ad was duly located among the various personal notices in the back of the previous week's paper.

"Here it is!" Lionel, now barefoot after discarding his socks to prevent tripping over them, proceeded to read aloud the said ad, which was much longer than the usual brief "attractive young male seeks same" posts, in fact going on and on about the very *precise* and *exact* specifications required of all young applicants. Lionel read the ad out in a BBC newsreader voice while Elliot giggled softly.

"*And*," Lionel added, "here it is of *course*, the *sine qua non* at the end ... *Your underwear must be spotlessly clean!*"

"That lets *me* out!" admitted Elliot.

On that note, I headed for the bus.

I imagined Lord Piltdown's home to be a stately neo-Georgian row house like Marcus Grumbacher's—well-kept, with iron railings, well-manicured bushes, and a broad black front door with a brass knocker (Marcus's was an antique dolphin sporting an amiably wicked grin). It was instead a slightly

114

LONDON SKIN & BONES

forbidding three and a half story detached gray brick structure with an untidy front garden full of wheelbarrows, workmen's tools, and builder's waste. I was met at the door by Lord P himself—a more-or-less bald man of middle age and middle height with a protuberant nose, dressed in a conservative suit and iridescent flowered tie. He greeted me affably and waved me in, with assurances of how well recommended I was.

"Call me Geoffrey," he instructed—a small relief as I was unsure of the proper way to address a peer and had decided on "your lordship" though it seemed a mite formal. "I'll give you the grand tour," said Lord P, "and a cup of tea and then you can have a look at what's at stake."

The grand tour, with many stops and starts, asides and injunctions, took about half an hour. The main ground floor rooms were a sitting room and a library. My heart rather sank as we approached shelves crammed with government publications, legal volumes, and parliamentary speeches. But I was quickly assured that this was merely "my Working Library." My province was to be on one of the upper floors.

As we made our way through the house, my host explained that his "Private Library" was a modest one but needed to be "put in order." He murmured something about discretion and insurance. Much of the house was untidy and ill-used but its occupant was obviously fond of its varied contents. A wall in one room was adorned with a number of attractive small pictures. I peered at them and could not help noticing they needed a good dusting. Most of the decipherable signatures meant nothing to me but I was pleased to spot a Keith Vaughan, a tiny John Minton, and an odd, brightly colored abstract that proved to be by Gerald Wilde. On another wall was a larger blue and yellow painting by Tuke of happy, tousle-headed lads bathing by the sea in the altogether.

"The insurance on that one is ferocious," Lord P confided. "But it would break my heart to sell it. Reminds me of my childish days with my little spade and pail on the shores of the Wash!" He leaned toward me. "The Wash," he confided, "is quite *shallow*, you know." I expressed surprise. "I couldn't afford to buy these now," he confessed. "I'm so glad to have them." He turned to face me, beaming, pleased. His animated features and friendly manner had put me at ease and I ventured that on my own wall I had an etching of Charles Shannon by William Rothenstein, bought years before from a Toronto book dealer for next to nothing. *And* an Oswell Blakeston, a gift from the artist! Lord P seemed delighted to hear of these possessions, looking at me straight on and clapping me on both shoulders. "Wonderful!" he beamed. "You're off to a fine start!"

Basking in my host's approbation for a moment, I was able to get a proper look at both of his eyes at the same time. While the left eye fixed me amiably with a gray-blue stare, the clouded pupil of the right eye seemed at first to be looking off toward some distant corner of the room, then followed a slow, arc-like trajectory, ascending and descending like a leisurely passing moon, and coming to rest in a damp pool at the far corner of the eyelid. I noticed his face was mottled and bloodshot. Suddenly he remembered our ongoing tour and I followed his shuffling figure into a room full of cardboard boxes, some of which were overflowing with various leaflets and pamphlets in multiple copies.

"*These*," said Lord P with a certain emphasis, "are ..." (he extracted a pair of tracts with pictures of cows and bees on them) "from our Milk and Honey Society ... Do you know ... ?" I had to confess that I did not. He thrust the booklets into my hands. "I am a vegetarian, you know, and our Society does marvelous work *in the field.*" He paused. "That's not supposed to be a pun. Our *Outreach to Vegans*, you see. Do you know that vegans won't eat honey, the food of the gods? Or drink the Milk of Paradise either! Whatever would happen to the poor cows? The poor bees?" I could think of no reply but the question was apparently rhetorical. We made our way through the rest of the house, at one point climbing over small piles of flags, old weapons, war memorabilia, and insignia of various sorts. Eventually we reached a pleasant back room, the location of the uncatalogued books in question. Marcus had been right: the library was not a large one, just a modest bookcase or two, not, I was assured, arranged in any order. A desk and chair had been prepared for my use.

"I won't make you explore the belfry," my host assured me, indicating a set of stairs to the fourth floor attic. It's where I keep my cricket memorabilia. "*I never miss a season at Lord's you know,*" he added with pride, and the roving right eye once again wandered slowly in its arc like a lost planet. "*Bats in the belfry!*" he added with a grin—a small joke I expect he had made many times before. "I'll leave you to examine these while I make tea. I like to imagine myself an independent thinker," he added in slightly hushed tones, "and you'll find many of my interests represented here." And indeed I did.

I enjoy examining people's libraries and this promised to be one of the most intriguing. Books and pamphlets discussing curious and bizarre theories, odd takes on history, strange customs and obscure byways of

LONDON SKIN & BONES

thought were jumbled together in no order, some stuffed behind other books at the back of the shelves. They would need organizing as well as cataloguing. I jotted down some of the titles: *Churchill the Druid. The Eyes, Brain and Nerve System in Relation to the Earth's Magnetism. The Strange Story of False Teeth. Burmese Supernaturalism: A Study in the Explanation and Reduction of Suffering. World Nudism, the Key to World Peace.* I suspected *The Abominations of Modern Society* by Rev. T. De Witt Talmage might prove instructive ("It is but a short step from the ballroom to the graveyard!"). Here were books on UFOs, ley lines, tectonic plates, ice moons, lost gospels, lost tribes, the claims of the Jacobites, the Baconian cypher, the possible sites of Atlantis, the re-dating of Egyptian history and the arcane spiritual value of the Pyramid Inch. There were also some items of Uranian interest, including several plainly bound books of eyebrow-raising poems about boys by the Rev. E.E. Bradford, and a long anonymous essay, mimeographed and spiral bound, which seemed to extol the specific attractions of winsome lads in freshly laundered underwear. This bore the presumably bogus imprint "Hastings, Hither and Yon, 1972." I noticed one pamphlet that I'd read and reviewed not long before, a brief tract entitled *We Are All Androgynous Yellow*, by a disciple of one Dr. Charlotte Bach, an immigrant Hungarian with unusual ideas about human sexuality and evolution.

"Do you know Dr. Charlotte Bach?" my host asked. "A behemoth of a woman with a man's voice and impenetrable theories. She spoke at our club a while back," he added. "Impossible to understand! Only thing I remember is she described Eldridge Cleaver as a parasite on the body of the undead. I didn't argue *that* point." He waved a hand in dismissal. "I can't have anything to do with frauds or hoaxes of any sort," he added, firmly and improbably. "I'm rather afraid of it. I have my reputation to think of."

Soon I was left alone with the library and made a start on crafting order out of chaos. Pens, pencils, a typewriter, and cellophane-wrapped packets of file cards had been thoughtfully provided. At one point in the afternoon, a middle-aged factotum in a waiter's jacket appeared bearing a tray with a stack of Marmite and cucumber sandwiches, a large pot of Earl Grey tea, flanked by milk and honey, and a tempting slab of pink and white coconut ice.

"His Lordship thought you might like a bite to eat."

I never saw the man in the waiter's jacket again, then or on any of the visits I made to complete the job. After a few hours I was ushered out, and a date set for my next appearance. As I was leaving, I remarked on an odd

117

IAN YOUNG

artifact in the front hall that I hadn't noticed when I came in. It appeared to be a painted, plaster replica of a bald human head in a glass case.

"I'm sure you've heard of Piltdown Man," said my host. I knew of the so-called Piltdown Skull of course—bone fragments found in a Sussex gravel pit, alleged to be the remains of the fabled Missing Link and then, forty years on, exposed as a fake. "A relic of a half-forgotten scandal involving painted monkey parts. It did my family no good." Changing the subject, he mentioned Marcus Grumbacher's scholarly volumes on ancient coins and other numismatic subjects. "My grandfather, the first Earl, left me his coin collection, which he started with some old coins found on an excavation site. It's in a bank vault; I haven't looked at it in years. My father was always rather mysterious about it. Marcus encourages me to sell it; perhaps I should."

"If you do, take it to Marcus for evaluation," I suggested. "He's the best there is, so they say."

"So I understand. I really could use the money. And Marcus has done me a number of favours, not the least of which is providing the services of your good self. I must repay him somehow. You encourage me!"

I thought no more about it.

The next morning took me around the corner to the stamp shop as I wanted to retrieve Farouk's valise. Wondering what he had left me, I placed it on the big round table—it was quite heavy—and opened it with the key provided. It was packed with multiple copies of the same perfect-bound book entitled *Sexual Alternatives for Men: "Facts & Fantasies."* The dull, badly designed cover was a bilious green. Compiled by John S. Barrington and published by something called The Alternative Publishing Company, its two hundred plus pages crammed with eye-straining type detailed various homo- and bisexual "case histories," interspersed with pseudo-scholarly ramblings and crudely produced charts. I wondered what I should do with it.

By the time I decided to phone my friend Roger Baker, an editor with various gay magazines, I had disposed of two copies: one in Boris's window and another in his counter display alongside various stamp books and stray leaflets. I gave Boris a third copy for himself, which he vowed he would begin that very evening, "in bed—with my Ovaltine."

I had barely begun to describe my windfall to Roger when it became clear he knew the volume in question all too well. Apparently, Barrington, whose reputation was as a physique photographer rather than a scientific researcher, had printed the book at his own expense, hoping to reap a

LONDON SKIN & BONES

huge profit. Things hadn't worked out quite that way, Roger informed me. Barrington had offered copies to every bookshop and gentlemen's goods emporium in and around Charing Cross Road. Most of them weren't keen on it, he said, but "a few of them have it in the window next to the trusses and *A History of the Lash*. Not the bestseller he was hoping for."

Leaving most of the books with Boris, I headed to the only enterprise in Finsbury Park that might just be a possible retail customer, Joe Polidori's Tobacco. The sign said just Tobacco, but Joe sold newspapers, magazines, a few books, and all sorts of odd items, with skin books, gay and straight, on a discreet rack in the back, alongside tarts' advertisements pinned to a cork board. I was halfway through my pitch when Joe indicated a small stack of books in a corner. Among them were several copies of *Sexual Alternatives for Men*.

"I can't move them," he admitted. "And I'm stuck with a box of them. Now if they had some proper photographs ..."

Back at the boarding house on Turle Road that evening, I was sitting at the kitchen table making my way through *Sexual Alternatives* when Andy Boom came in to make a cup of tea—shirtless in jeans and braces. I had already lost interest in the book when Andy set himself down across the table from me, his smooth, almost hairless chest and bushy armpits far more engaging than Mr. Barrington's turgid prose.

"Epping Forest tomorrow!" he reminded me.

We had agreed to venture into the Forest, weather permitting, to a spot I favored near the Great Hart pub. I always enjoyed going to the Forest, just to relax, explore, and mooch about. One weekend I had persuaded Andy to join me and as it happened, we had come across a group of children, mostly boys, operating little remote-powered speedboats on one of the ponds. Andy became engrossed in the speedboats and was always eager to sit and watch them a while.

"It's the competition this Sunday," Andy informed me. "For the Lord Tod Wadley Cup!"

I didn't have much interest in the Lord Tod Wadley Cup but was just pleased to be going to the Forest with Andy.

"I like Epping Forest," he said. "There's always a place to piss."

This remark made me remember Farouk's parting injunction the previous morning. Savoring a mouthful of tea I tried to stifle a laugh—and failed, snorting the tea out of both nostrils, all over the table.

IAN YOUNG

"Bloody hell," Andy muttered, unconcerned, and mopped up the mess I'd made with a tea-towel bearing Union Jacks and pictures of Prince Charles and Lady Di.

Hours later I woke up in the middle of the night, feeling cold. It was a sad fact of the Turle Road house that each room had its own heating system, if you could call it that, the amount of warmth allocated determined by how many 50p coins had been deposited in an antique-looking meter. I climbed into my flannel dressing gown, took a coin from a small, diminishing pile, dropped it into the slot—CLANG!—and padded to the bathroom. At some point during my peripatetics, it suddenly occurred to me where I might have seen Lord Piltdown's manservant before. Hadn't he been the driver of the car that had whisked Farouk Wylie away from the front of Boris's shop? I was almost sure of it! I climbed into bed, pulled the blankets around me, and was soon asleep.

It was several months later that a hefty package turned up in the mail, propped against my door by Russell, our landlord. I opened it to find a large, lavishly illustrated catalogue printed in Singapore on heavy stock. The cover depicting several old coins read:

Marcus A. Grumbacher Numismatics
&
Europa—De Lisle Auctions
present
A Unique Collection:
Twenty-five Centuries of
Classic Counterfeit Coins

Usually, auction catalogs boast of the provenance of their contents but this collection remained anonymous. Tucked inside my copy was a textured off-white card bearing the familiar image of a grinning antique dolphin and the engraved message: With the Compliments of Marcus A. Grumbacher. Marcus had written my name across the card in his old-fashioned copperplate, and beneath it, "This collection from a Peer of the Realm did very well. Again, my thanks!"

Boris sold both his copies of *Sexual Alternatives for Men*, but the rest of the books were passed along to friends. I gave one to Lord Piltdown—Geoffrey—who said he was awfully pleased.

ONE FOR THE OLD SARGE

"Why do they call him the Old Sarge anyway?" Russell asked. "He's not *that* old!"

"Don't you know?" said Andy. "Don't you read *Gay News*?" Andy, a young skinhead with ideas of his own, resisted calling himself "gay" but was an avid reader of *Gay News*, a fortnightly paper that published my reviews and photographs now and then, earning me a few extra Pounds.

It was evening and we were in the back garden of the boarding house on Turle Road, hanging around between the herb garden and the chicken coops. Russell Hicks, our landlord, was an amiable chap approaching forty, blond, bespectacled, well fleshed out, the man you'd overlook in a crowd. As a very young man he had gone to Australia to make his fortune, which, as it happened, he did. He had turned his talents to the art of the con, moving from city to city enticing people out of their money by means of what he called "the blind guide dog racket." The premise of the con was a simple one: "Our guide dogs have helped blind people all their lives. No longer sighted, now they need YOUR help. Won't you contribute some small amount ..." The idea, he said, had come to him after he had rescued Sarah, a blind Alsatian bitch, from the pound. He and Sarah had run the scheme in various Australian centers for years apparently. Eventually Sarah died at a great age and Russell returned to the land of his birth, fortune in hand. He had made enough to put a substantial deposit on the old row house on Turle Road. Rooms were rented out as "Holiday Flats" to get around the draconian rental regulations which made it virtually impossible to evict anyone for any reason.

We had come out to check on the chickens, which had been acting strangely, but they seemed to have calmed down. Russell picked one up and began stroking her as she appeared to fall asleep in his arms.

"It's the Old Sarge because of his personal ads for buddies in *Gay News*," Andy explained. "The ones that start 'Report for Duty!' or 'Attention Soldier!' That sort of thing. The military discipline scene. All fun and games, all signed The Old Sarge."

I remembered the first time I'd encountered him before I moved to Finsbury Park and ended up working for him selling clothes and boots from the racks and shelves of his military surplus shop. I was in the Carousel Club one night, hoping to spot someone congenial. I noticed a well-built middle-aged man with close-cropped graying hair, leaning against the wall in a dark corner. The flash of a match as he lit a cigar showed a sympathetic face with a puckish grin, and he was looking right at me.

I was certainly being cruised, but I generally don't fancy older men and in any case I was soon whisked away to one of the gaudily painted booths by the journalist Roger Baker who was eager to buy me a drink and talk shop. I didn't see Sarge again until after I had settled into my Finsbury Park lodgings, a couple of blocks from his place of business.

My first evening in the Park had been rainy and miserable. I walked across the darkened parking lot of the George Orwell Secondary School next to my new home. At that point I knew nobody in the district and was already having second thoughts about moving all the way from Canada to what seemed a perennially impoverished England. I was feeling rather sorry for myself as I made my way to the house, and the clang, clang, clang of chains against the metal poles in the schoolyard echoed my low spirits.

This all seemed far away now, and my fears of a bleak existence had been overtaken by modest but comfortable quarters, some new friends, and a decently paying job with the Old Sarge, who had made no mention of our brief near-encounter when he hired me to staff the shop and "learn the ropes."

My self-centered ruminations were interrupted by the arrival of the local Vicar, the Rev. Dr. Ralph Menzies-Cholmondeley (pronounced I must add in the British manner, "Rafe Mingiss-Chumley") but always just referred to as the Vicar, also in the British manner. The Vicar was a slight man with an expansive forehead and black, slicked-back hair, who wore sunglasses most of the time, due, he said, to an eye condition. He had come to collect a

"The flash of a match as he lit a cigar showed he was looking right at me"

dozen eggs from Russell's chickens. He was in fact the coop's only customer, the remaining productions ending up on our kitchen table in one form or another.

"Some of the cats like these," said the Vicar, fingering an egg with a broad grin. Various feral and stray cats made their home in part of his churchyard, supervised and fed by the Vicar and one or two neighbors.

He turned to Russell, remembering some earlier conversation. "I recommended that very nice lady to the Bishop as part-time help. He seemed grateful but he did ask whether she believed in God. I said I thought she did but she didn't believe in the Bible. Oh, said the Bishop, that's all right then. There are so many atheists about now one can't be too careful." The Vicar put his carton of eggs into a wicker cat-basket and scuttled away.

Russell's question had turned my thoughts to Sarge himself. When he hired me he said he needed someone to put his records in order and I soon found out how shockingly true that was. I had emerged from the ruins of what had once appeared to be a promising academic career and had been working at the London and Manchester Sanitary Packing Goods Company, a friendly, inefficient business paying absurdly low wages. So I was glad to accept the offer of a significant raise in pay and a job I could easily do. Sarge showed me the basics of the business, and his mongrel dog Soldier adopted me as friend and dogwalker. I wondered about my new employer's rasping, hacking cough. But England's damp, chilly climate meant that many of its inhabitants had a tendency to spit up phlegm much of the time, nursing a checklist of bronchial ailments.

The Sarge was usually to be found behind the counter at the front of the shop, perched on a high stool or leaning on the counter with a cloth in his hand, cleaning and polishing the glass case where various badges, knives, and other bits of militaria were displayed. This habitual stance reminded me of a bartender and once I asked him whether he had ever tended bar.

"Oh, yes!" he said. "That's how I got this." He indicated the long, white scar that ran from his temple to his chin. "They cut me up. I'll tell you all about it sometime." But Sarge was a man of few words, and revelations about his past were rare.

I generally worked in the back of the shop where the cast-off uniforms and footwear of a dozen armies were arrayed on shelves and in racks and bins. My employer, an easy man to work for, had a shrewd business sense, a friendly way with the customers, and a valuable ability to ease them out of

LONDON SKIN & BONES

the front of the shop and into the street when necessary. If they started to get obstreperous with one another, Sarge would fix them with a glance and the much repeated suggestion, "If you boys are going to fight, put on jockstraps!" ("Inside every bad boy," he used to say, "there's a good boy trying to get out. And inside every good boy, there's a bad boy trying to get out!")

Over the months we worked together, folding battle-dress trousers or sorting singlets (the West German ones with the eagle on them were the most popular), Sarge would fill me in on such essentials as how to work with suppliers and the best ways to display merchandise. He told me there was no point in indicating the national origin of any item unless it's British or American, as they're the only ones customers care about.

Unlike most of the people I knew in the district, Sarge wandered far afield, frequenting various pubs and gay clubs, and driving his van around at night, usually with a helper, to scavenge any likely items put out for rubbish pickup. I accompanied him once or twice on these outings and was surprised at the good things people throw out.

I was certainly more content working at Sarge's Military Surplus than I ever had been studying philosophy and English. Still, I couldn't help wondering where if anywhere it would all lead, and if I had done the right thing jumping (or falling) off the academic wagon at a great university just to end up folding discarded trousers in Finsbury Park. These mixed feelings accompanied me to a weekend visit to my friends, the Andrews family, in Ongar.

After a weekend of hospitality, food and music, I got back to the house on Turle Road late on Sunday evening, carrying a bag of magazines from the Andrews household and half a dozen mince tarts from the Andrews' neighbor Aunt Doll, a thanks for helping set up her teacup reading booth at the church fete. I had avoided having my tea leaves read. My past may be an open book but I prefer my future to be a closed one.

I walked down the hall. Russell was in the kitchen, washing cups.

"Bad news, mate," he said, putting the tea towel down and pulling out a chair. My first thought was that he'd be giving up the house, but I was wrong. "Sarge had an accident. He's dead."

I was silent for a few seconds before asking what happened.

"Fell down the stairs. They think he had a heart attack."

I had always felt that if the Old Sarge fell ill, it would be something to do with his nasty cough, but this was quite unexpected. I could only sit and

125

stare at Russell as he sipped his tea from an oversized drinking mug adorned with a picture of a dog in dark glasses and the words "Blind Guide Dog Fund—Brisbane." The small world I had settled into had just shifted. In the few days that followed, I opened up Sarge's Military Surplus every workday, walked Sarge's dog, and carried on as before. The daze I was in lasted until the funeral, a modest, private service as requested, followed by a well-attended wake at Ali's Café. There, watching Russell slurping his mug of tea, I suddenly flashed on his Blind Guide Dog mug at home.

"You didn't bring that dog mug from Australia, did you?" I asked irrelevantly.

"No," he explained patiently, "I did not. I had it made up here. Reminds me of Sarah and my former life."

We reminisced about the Sarge for a while and I remembered he'd once said he'd like to have his ashes scattered on Boudicca's grave on Hampstead Heath.

"It's not really her grave, is it?" I asked naïvely.

"No, of course not," said Russell. "During the War they put a couple of anti-aircraft guns up on the Heath, it's a high spot, you see. The bigger one they called Boudicca but they pronounced it Boa-da-see-ya in those days. Got a direct hit with a bomb that blew it to pieces and the site's been Boudicca's grave ever since."

The things you learn!

Boris Mostayenko, stamp dealer and old friend to the Sarge, joined us at the table.

"We're to go to Marcus Grumbacher's Saturday," he said. "News of the Sarge's estate—nothing to worry about." He patted me on the wrist, cigarette ash peppering the table. It was all a little mysterious but hearing Marcus was involved gave me confidence. A few days later I rode with Boris on the upstairs of a double-decker bus to Hampstead.

As well as being a numismatic expert, Marcus was a successful real estate speculator, owning, among other properties, the buildings that housed both Sarge's and Boris's shops. I had visited him a few times on various errands, and had learned bits and pieces of his unusual past. He was born in Vaduz in the Principality of Liechtenstein to an old banking family, traditional financial advisers to the ruling Princes. As a young man he had been stationed in post-War Vienna with an international organization helping refugees. The very young Boris Mostayenko had made his way there from

LONDON SKIN & BONES

Prague, hoping to find a new home somewhere in the West. Marcus had apparently employed some mysterious government contacts to bring him safely to England.

Marcus himself was a man of about sixty, squarely built, tending to stoutness, with a full head of silver hair, a way of walking that made him seem to glide across the carpeted floor, and a quiet, authoritative voice that sounded calm and reassuring, almost hypnotic. The ground floor of his Georgian-style house in Hampstead served as his place of business. It was there, surrounded by bookshelves and tanks of slow-moving tropical fish, and watched over by an oversized oil painting of the composer Rheinberger, that Boris and I sat in leather-covered armchairs sipping excellent coffee from dainty china cups, and listening intently as a sheaf of legal papers was placed before us.

Marcus was, at it turned out, the executor of the Old Sarge's estate, such as it was. The Sarge was a frugal man and had left his few personal possessions and a small amount of money to be divided between Boris and a relative living in Southend. The building housing Sarge's shop and upstairs living quarters, remained, of course, Marcus's property. I had expected to be bequeathed Sarge's amiable dog Soldier and perhaps some small item or a few books. Instead I was surprised to hear that Sarge had left me not only his dog but his business as well. The fate of Sarge's Military Surplus now lay in *my* hands.

As Marcus and Boris conferred, I sat in silence, thinking back to the first time I had seen Sarge in the Carousel Club, his friendly grin illuminated in a dark corner by the light of a cigar. And of his subsequent kindness. Now the extent of his friendship for me made me feel a bit ashamed that I hadn't made my gratitude more obvious.

In an hour, our talk ended, we finished our coffees, and returned to Finsbury Park, not on the bus, but in a taxi which Marcus arranged and paid for. I didn't open up the shop right away but walked through the dusty streets of the Park and sat for a few minutes on the bench outside Mrs. Singh's laundrette. Over the past few weeks I had been mulling over my circumstances. After my first dreary night in the district I had managed to pick myself up after a fashion. I considered myself lucky. And now I felt I'd been given a stake in my own future. I had an actual business to run! As well as an obligation to the Old Sarge to stay on and make a go of things. The overcast morning had turned into a sunny afternoon and as I sat, mulling over my jumbled feelings of gratitude, grief, regret, and resolution, the Vicar, the Reverend Doctor Ralph Menzies-Cholmondeley, protector of stray cats, shuffled into view. I walked with him toward High Street and he commiserated with me on the death of my friend and employer.

"He was very good to me," I said. "I owe him a lot."

"What a good man," the Vicar murmured. "Of course, you know ..." At that point he paused to look straight at me through his dark glasses.

"Know what?" I inquired.

"Oh, my goodness! Oh, my dear." He became thoughtful and perhaps a little nervous. "Well ... Do you have a few moments? Perhaps ..."

As he seemed reluctant to further our talk on the public street, I suggested we continue around the corner to my Turle Road lodgings. We went into the kitchen to make tea which we could take upstairs to my room. As it happened, that afternoon the kitchen was crowded with housemates. Andy, the two cooks from the middle floor, and Christopher, the handsome student we seldom saw, crowded around the table. Soldier was sleeping and twitching in a basket by the door. Our landlord Russell was in his element, standing at the head of the table, holding forth like a fairground barker, several playing cards splayed before him on the arborite tabletop.

"I'm showing them the four-card standup!" he explained to his new arrivals. "It's a bit like three-card monte, only there are—that's right, *four cards*, Oh, you're a bright lot!—*four cards* and I don't need an accomplice, it's all straight up sleight of hand! I'm going to show you the trick. And *then*," he added with delight, *"I'm going to show you how it's done!"*

The boys looked on intently, eager to be let in on the arcane mysteries of the four-card stand-up. The Vicar appeared as curious as the rest. Polishing his sunglasses with a handkerchief, he leaned forward so as not to miss a single gesture, his little eyes gleaming darkly.

"Are you ready?" asked Russell, grinning broadly. We were ready. I was soon engrossed along with the others, the promise of gossipy revelations temporarily forgotten. The kettle began to boil, the teabags were in the mugs. Whatever the Vicar might want to tell me would have to wait for just a few more minutes.

ABOUT THE AUTHOR

Ian George Young was born at St. Bartholomew's Hospital, London (where Holmes met Watson) on January 5, 1945, during a severe air raid ("I call it the night Hitler tried to kill me"). He has been active in the Peace, Civil Rights, Gay Liberation, and AIDS Dissident movements, and founded the first gay literary press, Catalyst. His books include *Sex Magick, The Stonewall Experiment: A Gay Psychohistory, The Male Muse, Out in Paperback: A Visual History of Gay Pulps, The Male Homosexual in Literature: A Bibliography,* and *Encounters with Authors.* An avid stamp collector, he is an occasional contributor to the philatelic press. He lives in Toronto with his partner, Wulf.

CPSIA information can be obtained
at www.ICGtesting.com
Printed in the USA
LVOW10s1617231017
553452LV00010B/925/P